NETFLIX

STRANGER THINGS

HAWKINS HORRORS

A COLLECTION OF TERRIFYING TALES

Cover illustrated by Patrick Spaziante

Original cover photo used with kind permission of Joe Hiltabidel Photography.

Copyright © 2022 by Netflix Inc. All rights reserved. Published in the United States by Random House Children's Books, a division of Penguin Random House LLC, New York. Random House and the colophon are registered trademarks of Penguin Random House LLC. Stranger Things and all related titles, characters, and logos are trademarks of Netflix Inc.

ReadStrangerThings.com

ISBN 978-0-593-48396-1 (trade)—ISBN 978-0-593-48397-8 (ebook)

Printed in the United States of America

10 9 8 7 6 5 4 3

First Edition 2022

Random House Children's Books supports the First Amendment and celebrates the right to read.

NETFLIX

STRANGER THINGS

HAWKINS HORRORS

A COLLECTION OF TERRIFYING TALES

Matthew J. Gilbert

RANDOM HOUSE 🏠 NEW YORK

CONTENTS

11:58 P.M.

Midnight was rapidly approaching.

They needed to get to Steve and Robin before it was too late.

"Step on it, will ya? Time's a-wastin'!" Dustin shouted.

"Don't shout at me," Nancy shot back. "I'm going the speed limit. We have children in the car!"

Erica poked her head into the front seat. "Are you talking about me?"

"Yes. I'm talking about all of you," Nancy said, eyes in the rearview mirror. She scanned the faces of Lucas, Erica,

Max, and Dustin. They all looked back at her—a lineup of impatient faces crammed into the backseat. "You guys are acting like this is a life-and-death situation."

Like a chorus, they replied in unison: "It is."

"It is," Mike added, fidgeting in the passenger seat next to her. He tapped the clock on the car's dashboard. "We've only got two minutes! Here's the turn!"

"I know where it is!" Nancy said, cutting the wheel hard.

With the squeal of rubber, the Wheeler family car came careening out of the darkness. It nearly clipped the curb veering into the parking lot of the Hawkins strip mall. During the day, this place was buzzing with shoppers, skaters, and hellraisers of all ages, but the car's headlights told a different story right now.

At midnight, everything looked like it was covered by a blanket of inky shadows. Even the revolving sign for the Palace Arcade had gone dark. The streetlights flickered weakly until they suddenly died, succumbing to a massive power outage that was wreaking havoc across all of Hawkins.

It was a total blackout for miles. And it had happened in

a matter of seconds. The kids were so focused on speeding to the video store, they hadn't noticed the shadowscape that awaited them.

Nancy turned in and stopped next to the only other car in the desolate parking lot: a purple BMW. Harrington's.

Dustin had his face wedged against the backseat window, but he could still see the familiar ride through the condensation on the glass. "Thank Christ, they're still here! Let's go!"

The kids stumbled out of the car even before the engine could wheeze to a stop. One by one they lined up, knocking on the glass doors of their secret meeting place: the epicenter of culture and entertainment for miles around, a sanctuary for outcasts, and a place of salvation from a weekend doomed to boredom.

FAMILY VIDEO

Within moments, the silhouette of someone perfectly coiffed came to the door and unlocked it.

"What have I told you savages about banging on the windows?" Steve asked, suddenly illuminating his face with a flashlight.

3

They all gave him the obligatory apology before dropping the courtesy and pushing their way past him into the video store.

"Why's it all dark? Did the lights just go out?" Nancy asked, locking the car.

Steve held the door for her. "Literally *just* happened like five minutes ago. Robin and I were about to bail."

"What about the midnight movie?"

"That's the thing about VCRs, Nance. They don't turn on when there's no power. Crazy, huh?"

"Someone got up on the wrong side of the hair spray today."

"*Someone* has been restocking while *someone else* has been pretending to restock."

He meant Robin, who was currently sitting on the front-desk countertop, a flashlight in one hand and a package of red rope licorice in the other. She gave Nancy a wave as she entered the shadowy video store.

"Welcome to the video store . . . ," Robin said in a spooky, deep voice, "AT THE END OF THE WORLD!" Then she dropped the voice and perked up, all bubbly. "Candy?"

"Red licorice?" Nancy asked.

4

"I couldn't pry the popcorn machine open," Robin replied.

"It doesn't just open when the power goes out," Steve said. "It's not a safe. And this isn't a heist movie."

Dustin pulled out a tiny flashlight on his key chain. "Speaking of movies, what's the plan for tonight?"

"*Ghostbusters*?" Lucas asked, hopeful.

"No! Not again," Max piped up. "I was gonna see if you guys had gotten *Cat's Eye* yet?"

"A kitty-cat movie," Erica said, dismissive. "I was hoping for something Rated R. You promised Rated R."

"Sorry," Lucas said to the group. "Mom and Dad are out of town. I had to bring her, and certain promises were made."

Max laughed. "It's not a kids' movie about cats. It's a horror anthology of different Stephen King stories. It's supposed to be wild!"

"Well, that hardly matters now. Hello? We have no power," Steve reminded them.

"We could still do the scary-story thing," Mike suggested. "Might not be Stephen King level, and Drew Barrymore's not involved. But we can still get good and scared. Besides, what

5

the hell else are we gonna do till the lights come back on?"

"We could clean up," Robin suggested. A moment later, she added: "Kidding, guys. Sheesh. Tough room."

"All right, let's have it: anyone got a good scary story?" Steve asked.

Erica couldn't believe what she was hearing. "Now you want *us* to tell scary stories? I come to the video store to be entertained, not the other way around," she said.

"What are you more afraid of, Erica? That we're telling scary stories?" Steve asked, turning off his flashlight for effect. "Or that we're telling them . . . *in the dark*?"

Silence. They all looked at one another for the next few moments, almost afraid to make a sound. Though no one could quite put it into words, there was something *terrifying*, on a deeply human level, about saying what you feared out loud when there was barely a beam of light to cut through. It was as if the darkness could somehow make those fears *real*.

"I've got one," Nancy finally said from behind one of the shelves. "I've been researching Pennhurst lately, for a piece I'm doing for the paper, and the stuff that happens there would make your skin crawl."

That got Robin's attention. "Pennhurst? The place up the road?"

"Oh, it's not just some place up the road. It's a hospital for the criminally insane. About five or so minutes away from here. It's been around for decades. The most violent inmates in Hawkins, all under one roof."

"Okay, I changed my mind. This sounds *good*," Erica said, taking some red rope licorice and sitting back against the shelves. She was ready to be entertained. "Terrify me."

Everyone in the group got comfortable, as Nancy had the floor. She borrowed Dustin's flashlight and illuminated her face from underneath for effect.

"What I'm about to tell you is one hundred percent real. It's a matter of county record. It's been documented by serious journalists and investigated by state and local authorities, yet still remains *unsolved*. It happened one night, on a night just like this, back in 1969. A patient complained about hearing..."

7

A LiTTLe VoiCe

What do you think of when you hear the words *Pennhurst Asylum*?

A home for the criminally insane?

A dark prison for someone like Jimmy Ray Cutts?

After Cutts killed seven innocent people, he told the police he had no memory of committing the crimes. He swore that someone else—some*thing* else—had been pulling his strings that night. Like everyone else nearby, Christina had heard the stories and mostly ignored them. She didn't believe in ghosts and demons, but she did believe in monsters—just not the kind you see in rubber masks, in the movies. The monsters she saw were simply broken human beings in need of serious mental care. They could look as normal as your neighbors, your coworkers, even your boss.

Christina was surrounded by so-called maniacs six days a week—it was her job. She was a nurse-in-training. Sometimes, when she rode the bus to work, she'd hear kids scaring each other about the asylum up the road where she spent most of her time. They'd whisper, "Monsters live in Pennhurst."

Well, she knew people like Ricky Dobbs also lived there.

Ricky was just a nineteen-year-old kid. Boyishly handsome, with his winning smile and athletic frame, he looked like one of those quarterbacks who were always surrounded by reporters on TV. His laugh was contagious, and like a child, he found the simplest things funny, like someone dropping their clipboard, or the way certain words, like lickety-split, sounded when they were slowly pronounced out loud.

Lick-et-eeee-split, he'd say repeatedy, stretching the word out more each time. *Liiiiick-etttt-eeeeee-spliiiiiit.* Fits of laughter followed.

Ricky wasn't a monster. He kept his hands to himself and never tried to grab Christina's hair. And he didn't have to be as heavily medicated as some of the more extreme cases on his block. Which meant he could speak, unlike the zombies. That was what Christina called the tranquilized group—the ones who needed a sedative just to function day-to-day in the asylum.

Ricky was no zombie, and he didn't seem crazy. He was just immature and shy.

And Christina would know. She'd been looking in on him for six months straight now, six nights a week, like clockwork, on the graveyard shift.

Christina was twenty-two years old. Pennhurst was her first job after college, and she was determined to do her best. Her responsibilities included patrolling the hallways at night. She had to look in on each patient on her list and make sure they were okay. She'd check each patient off, wait two hours, and do it again.

Rinse. Repeat.

Clean the nurse's office. Restock meds. Take her nightly stroll.

Observe. Check. Report. Check.

Watch the clock. Dream of sleeping in on Sunday morning. Sneak a candy bar.

Walk. Check. No one hurt. Check. No danger. Check.

This was Christina's life—until she finished her probationary period and became a full-fledged Pennhurst nurse. Then she'd get a raise, a locker, and the coveted right to choose her own shift hours.

One morning, as the first rays of sun sliced through the clouds, the senior staff started appearing in the hallways in a sea of white coats. It was time for them to take the reins from the night crew.

"All patients are healthy and accounted for," Christina told the head hurse. Then she packed up her things and headed for the exit.

But not before stopping to look in on Ricky Dobbs one more time.

She peeked through the bars of his door but saw only an empty bed. Her eyes searched the room, but there was no sign of Ricky. She was about to call for one of the senior nurses, when she heard a whimpering voice.

"Okay, okay, I promise. I'll do it—"

It was Ricky's voice.

Christina unlocked his room and slowly opened the door.

"Shhh!" she heard Ricky say as he jumped up, startled. He was tall and muscular but acted like a little boy who'd been caught doing something he shouldn't have been doing. Christina saw that he had been in the corner, against the wall. A perfect spot for hiding from the staff's two-inch-by-two-inch view of his room.

"You're up early," Christina said in a friendly manner.

"I don't have a watch." Ricky smiled. "I don't really know what time it is."

"Were you talking to someone just now?"

"What's the problem here?" a white coat asked, storming in. It was a doctor, one of the stuffy ones. Christina always forgot his name. Fortunately, he was wearing a name tag: SPEARS.

"And why are *you* not in restraints?" Dr. Spears observed, shoving his way past Christina. He called for support and two beefy orderlies filed in, instantly grabbing Ricky's arms, forcing them to his sides. Ricky protested a bit as they moved him back toward the bed, which was bolted to the wall.

"Ow, you're hurting me!" Ricky cried.

"No, wait, there's no problem at all, Dr. Spears," Christina said. "I was just—"

"Why was this patient not restrained?" Dr. Spears interrupted accusingly. He motioned for Christina to follow him out into the hall. Crestfallen, she looked at Ricky, trying to fight back from the orderlies' grip. This was all her fault. If only she'd kept going, he wouldn't be straining underneath the weight of a pair of three-hundred-pound men. She'd merely wanted to make sure he was okay.

"Dobbs hasn't been in restraints since I started here," she protested. "He's a trusted patient who never causes any trouble. Please—"

"So there were no special instructions given to you last night?"

"No, sir."

"Then someone else is in trouble. Because I left explicit instructions for senior staff to let night crew know that starting now, all patients are to be restrained at night. No matter their threat."

"May I ask why? Has something happened?"

"Jimmy Ray Cutts."

Christina felt a chill down her back.

"It's been five years since his infamous killing spree," Dr. Spears continued. "It's an unholy anniversary, an invitation to madness. There's chaos in the air, and that chaos will be like the scent of blood to the ravenous pack of filth under this roof. They'll want to impress him. They'll try to get his attention, to commemorate his evil deeds. I won't allow it. Cutts is being kept under twenty-four-hour surveillance, in protected custody, for the next few weeks. I will have Hawkins police here to keep the peace. I advise you to stay vigilant. These people are not your friends, they are our patients. And for their safety, and yours, I expect you to restrain *every one of them* from now on."

In an even graver tone, he added: "Things are about to get very interesting around here."

The next night, Christina went to work a little earlier than usual. She'd been worried about Ricky all day, unable to sleep, especially after Spears's bizarre speech, which made it sound like Pennhurst was about to turn into some sort of war zone. She half expected to be frisked by an officer of Hawkins PD when she went through the double doors.

But all was quiet.

The guard who normally checked her in wasn't at his desk. No signs of orderlies or other staff in the main hallway. Was there a staff meeting she'd forgotten to report to? *Maybe it's someone's birthday,* she thought. *They're probably all hiding back in the staff room, stuffing themselves with cake and punch.*

She could have followed up on this—she liked cake as much as the next person. It would be easy to pick up the duty phone to confirm that this imagined birthday party was real, but all that went through her mind at that moment was *Be quiet.*

This was her chance to check on Ricky before the hustle and bustle of lights-out began. She didn't even stop to hang up her jacket.

She went directly to Ricky Dobbs's cell.

Her shoes squeaked on the freshly buffed linoleum floor, the sounds hitting faster and faster as her steps became brisker and shorter. She passed a cell, and then another. Ricky's door was in sight.

And from here, she could see . . . it was open.

"AAAHHHHH!!!" An orderly screamed, running from the room, frantic. His footsteps boomed along the floor. His white uniform was splattered with blood, and his hand covered his face. He took a few steps, then fell to the floor with a smack. A nurse soon appeared in the hallway and ran to his side.

Shocked, Christina was barely able to croak, "What's going on?"

The other nurse was too busy to answer. Christina stepped forward to get a good look into Ricky's room.

It looked like a crime scene.

For a moment, time stood still. Christina couldn't hear the people yelling; she could only hear the thunderous pounding of her own heart.

A man was lying on the floor, surrounded by doctors and nurses. From this angle, Christina could tell he was badly hurt, but she couldn't tell exactly *how*. Judging by the puddle of blood, he was certainly fighting for his life. Some of that terrible red was also splattered on the wall, like a stomach-churning art project. No one seemed to notice her. Everyone was caught up in the moment, trying to help the man. Trying to save him. Trying not to show fear in the face of certain death.

Her heartbeat normalized. She noticed the shoes of the injured man—pristine shoes, as white as bone. He was an orderly.

She was not looking at Ricky's blood. The injured orderly was there, lying on his back. His chest had been crushed by Ricky's bed frame. An ambulance was not going to make a difference.

"Hi," she heard Ricky say to her as the sound of the real world came rushing in. He said it calmly, like they had run into each other in Hawkins on a Saturday afternoon.

A police officer was holding him against the wall.

Ricky Dobbs had killed someone.

Christina was sure there'd been some mistake. Ricky couldn't have done this. She wanted to shout it from the rooftops to anyone who'd listen, but Spears and the other senior staffers kept her and the other skeleton crew sequestered in the supply room while they hammered out the details with the police. Christina ignored the chatter of the staff and tried to listen to Spears's statement.

The parts she heard at first were all things she already knew. "Ricky Dobbs was admitted for schizophrenia," Spears began. "Something about him . . . hearing voices from a very young age," and then he mumbled the next few words. "He has no immediate family and no local next of kin," Spears continued. He wanted Ricky to "remain under his care and direct supervision." Ricky had been showing "great progress on an experimental drug," but was now . . . *What was that last part?* . . . "complaining of hearing voices again."

Correction: *voice*, singular.

That was when Christina remembered her last interaction with him the previous shift: *It sounded like he'd been talking to someone.*

19

Was this something she should tell the cops? Her heart softened when she recalled how he said hi like he always did. Like there wasn't a horrific scene unfolding all around him.

The official story just doesn't make sense, Christina thought. They were making it seem like Ricky had been plotting to crush the orderly. Like he had knowingly loosened his bed frame over a few weeks and somehow set it *just right* so the mishap wouldn't appear suspicious.

Then he allegedly asked the orderly, "Would you look under my bed? I think I dropped my pill. . . ."

And when the orderly peeked under, Ricky supposedly pulled the frame off its hinges and slammed it down on him. Repeatedly.

Ricky couldn't have done that, Christina thought. *He doesn't even swat at the flies in the cafeteria.*

The other staffers started murmuring so much that Christina couldn't focus on eavesdropping. She could only hear the voices around her in the room.

"I heard a sound, so I came running. and that's when I saw him," a janitor said. Same old story.

"He had it out for that orderly," an elderly orderly piped up.

20

"Mick was his name. That patient wanted to get back at him for getting rough."

"I heard him saying someone told him to do it . . . but you know what I think? I think it was a crazy voice in his head told him," a security guard added.

We all have that little voice, don't we? Christina wanted to say. *That little voice that tells us to walk left when we should be walking right. To choose the shortcut over the road we know. Or to push that button that clearly says "Do not push." We've all heard our inner voice try to talk us out of a bad decision. A thought that spoke to you as clearly as a friend would on the phone.*

At that moment, Christina's little voice was speaking up.

She wanted to say all this to her coworkers, but she didn't. Her little voice—conscience . . . common sense . . . curse . . . whatever you want to call it—told her not to.

Christina simply sat in silence, waiting for her turn to see Ricky and get to the bottom of it all.

Later that shift, an emergency meeting was called, led by Spears, of course. He told the staffers that Hawkins police were allowing Ricky to remain in Pennhurst while they began their investigation into the homicide of Michael "Mick" Hogan, the young orderly who'd died five minutes after Christina had seen him under Ricky's bed. She could have been imagining it, but Spears seemed almost pleased that this macabre chain of events had unfolded. Almost like it validated his doom-and-gloom speechifying from yesterday.

If anything, it gave Spears an excuse to keep all the patients tranquilized in a drug-induced state. All in the name of "keeping the peace," of course.

She'd never get an answer out of Ricky now. Not after a few cc's of "sleep juice."

During her rounds that night, Christina passed by Ricky's room, which was now sealed off with yellow crime scene tape. An aloof cop posted outside the door made sure no looky-loos snuck in to disturb the gory scene inside. She politely nodded and asked the officer where Ricky had been relocated.

"Room at the end of the hall," the cop answered.

As Christina made her way there, she could hear Ricky's voice. He was awake! She stepped a little lighter, a bit faster. She could hear him speaking in a low, raspy voice, but she couldn't quite make out the words.

She stopped outside the lookout bars of his new door, just in time to hear a gravelly voice say "Tomorrow . . . we'll get him . . ."

Only, it didn't sound like Ricky.

"Hey, new girl," someone said. Christina turned to see Sophia, a kind older nurse, coming around the corner with a syringe in her hand.

"Hey, Sophia, crazy night, huh?" Christina said.

"Nah," Sophia replied nonchalantly. "When you get to be here as long as I have, you see it all. You'll see, child. Murder isn't even a drop in the bucket. I've seen riots, escapes—"

"Escapes?"

Christina could barely hide her surprise . . . or was it excitement? Surrounded by all these white and gray bars, *escape* seemed like such a romantic notion. Like something out of a movie.

"Oh yeah," Sophia informed her. "Right before you started, we had a guy pull a Houdini in the middle of day shift. Didn't even take his shoes with him. Spears blew a gasket that day."

"How have I not heard about this?"

"It's not the kind of thing we like to be reminded about. Not our finest hour. Look, hon, I could sit here and tell you war stories all night," Sophia said, nursing her ankle and leaning against the wall. "But my dogs are barking from all the back-and-forth. I gotta sit down. Would you mind administering Ricky's knockout juice for me? My ankles are killing me."

Sophia offered her the needle.

"Of course, go sit down," Christina replied, doing her best to hide her excitement.

"Thanks, hon. Just take one of the guys with you. Can't be too careful," Sophia said, smiling at one of the muscle-bound orderlies nearby.

And with a nod of gratitude, Sophia unlocked the door to Ricky's room and let Christina in. The orderly followed, standing guard in the doorway.

"Hiiii . . . ," Ricky said, his voice trailing off. He was clearly a bit shaken up by the sight of another orderly.

"It's okay, Ricky," said Christina, offering him a smile. "I'm here to give you something to help you go to sleep."

Ricky pulled the blankets over his head, embarrassed. "I didn't mean it, you know? To hurt him. It wasn't supposed to hurt him so bad," he said, his voice quivering through the covers.

"I know, Ricky," Christina said. "Let me help you calm down now. I just need your arm."

Ricky's arm appeared from under the blanket. She could hear him sniffling while she held his hand and searched for a vein. Out of the corner of her eye, she saw the orderly suddenly peel off from the doorway to talk with another nurse.

She was finally alone with Ricky.

Now or never, Christina's little voice said. *Ask him. Something. Anything!*

"Ricky, just now, when I was coming in, I heard you talking, even though no one else is in here. And I noticed the same thing earlier this morning. Remember that? When you saw me and Dr. Spears come in with the guys?"

". . . Yeah, I guess . . ."

"Who were you talking to?"

"No one."

Christina prepped the tranquilizer shot, pushing the air out of the plunger until a little spray of solution came squirting out of the eye of the needle.

Christina tried again. "Were you maybe talking . . . to yourself? Because I do that sometimes too. We all do. It's normal."

Silence. She stuck him with the needle. He didn't make a peep.

"Okay, just lie down and you'll feel a little tired and then—"

"*Buck*," Ricky blurted out through the blanket. "He told me to call him *Buck*."

"Is that what you call the little voice in your head? You gave it a name?"

"He's not in my head. Not anymore. He's here with us."

Christina felt her pulse quicken. Something about the conviction in his voice, the faceless mass under the covers looking back at her . . . it was creepy. This was not how she'd envisioned this going at all.

Ricky went on. "He's a lot closer than you think."

She tightened up, feeling like the room was suddenly closing in on her.

"He sounds different now, as clear as you and I do," Ricky said through the blanket. "He tells me to do things. *Bad things.* I've never heard him like this."

Paralyzed with fear, Christina listened to Ricky's story as the rest of the world seemed to go quiet all around her. "He is *maaaad* . . . and you . . . don't . . . want him . . . *maaaaad*. . . . " His voice slowed. The drugs were clearly taking hold now.

"Or he'll come for you . . . *lick-et-eeeee* . . . *spliiii*—"

The mass under the covers suddenly fell back onto the bed, the mattress springs making him bounce a bit. Ricky was fast asleep, and all Christina could do was sit there and stare until the orderly returned.

27

The next few shifts were uneventful. Quiet, even.

The patients slept through most of the day and night, and the Hawkins police officers were rarely away from Jimmy Ray Cutts's cell in Pennhurst's East Wing.

The main hall, Christina's "beat," if you could call it that, felt like a ghost town. This was her chance to do a little digging.

Whenever Sophia and the other senior nurses would step out for their hourly smoke break, Christina would sneak into the office and secretly thumb through the patient records. It began as a search for info on Ricky's past, but that paperwork was long gone, most likely on the desk of some Hawkins deputy next to a half-eaten donut.

But one night something else caught her eye, and her imagination.

A red folder labeled FOR EXECUTIVE STAFF ONLY. SENSITIVE MATERIALS.

Normally, she would have shut the file cabinet and walked away, but a little voice in her head egged her on. There could be info in there about Ricky. Or significant dirt on Spears— hey, a girl could dream! She had to know what sinister secrets were inside the crimson folder. She grabbed it and quickly thumbed through the pages. It was a report on the escape of one "Harland Buck." The same infamous escape Sophia had mentioned. It read like the pages of a horror story.

An empty bed. Two empty shoes. An invisible man. He vanished into thin air.

It helped explain why Spears was so uptight. He'd lost a dangerous patient and could not have another major malfunction, especially with Jimmy Ray Cutts on the premises. She returned the file and got back to her official duties.

That was the night she noticed Ricky was *very interested* in the walls of his cell.

A few nights later, a storm hit Hawkins. It knocked down trees and made a mess of roadways. So much so that a lot of the senior Pennhurst staff were forced to stay on the grounds and wait out Mother Nature for their chance to return to their homes.

This meant the night shift and the senior day shift would spill over and walk the halls at the same time. Christina dreaded spending one minute extra with Spears. For a so-called sane man, he troubled her more than the "crazy" patients ever could.

As thunder clapped in the distance, Christina clocked her route to the med room, where Sophia, the only friendly nurse for ten miles, waited. "Hey, I'm here for Ricky's knockout juice," she said with a smile.

"Not tonight, hon." Sophia frowned. "Dr. Spears is stranded here because of the rain, and he wants to administer all of tonight's doses himself."

Christina got quiet and walked away. If she couldn't speak to Ricky tonight, she could at least still check in on him and make sure he was being treated responsibly. Like a person.

As she turned the corner, heading toward Ricky's cell, she heard Spears's voice in the distance. It started low and then shrieked loudly, echoing down the halls. Was he shouting over the roaring thunder that vibrated through the walls?

No, he was wailing. It sounded like—

"HEEEEEEELP!!!"

Right then, Christina saw a cluster of orderlies and guards crowding around the hall, trying to break down the door to Ricky's room. *"Help!"* she heard Spears bark from inside. He was barricaded in, and something was clearly blocking the door.

"What's going on?" Christina asked in a frenzy.

"Stay back!" one of the guards said, before ramming his shoulder into the door. It barely budged.

Christina couldn't see inside yet, but she could hear Spears's cries between the shouts of the orderlies.

–*"HEEEEEELP!"*–

"And let the cops know . . ."

–*"HEEEELP!"*–

". . . we got a situation here!"

An attendant sprinted off for help, and Christina took his place at the door. She peered through the lookout bars to see a tense scene inside. Ricky had removed his bed restraints and wrapped them around Spears's throat. The old man's pale pink face was turning purple.

Ricky continued to pull tighter and tighter.

But he wasn't enjoying himself.

In fact, he looked incredibly upset, tears streaking down

his cheeks. Christina didn't know what was going on, but she wanted to reason with him, if she could.

"Ricky, it's Christina!" she shouted. "Can you please let Dr. Spears go?"

"No!" Ricky yelled, distraught. "This is what Buck wants."

While Ricky continued to lock eyes with her, Spears managed to wriggle free. He pushed Ricky away long enough to cough air back into his lungs and pry the leather restraint guards off his neck. And then Christina saw the doctor do something no doctor should ever do.

In a fit of rage, Spears kicked Ricky in the ribs, knocking the wind out of him. Then he kicked him again and again. Then he unwedged the heavy bed frame barricading the door. The orderlies rushed in. One tended to Spears; the other restrained a tearful Ricky and called for a new knockout shot.

Christina was stunned. She froze as Spears walked past her, rubbing his throat. He wheezed orders: "Go to med check and get your friend his dose."

Christina returned to Sophia for a replacement syringe. On the outside, she was cool as a cucumber, but on the inside, she was fuming with anger. How dare Spears, a psychological professional, violate his oath and abuse a patient like that! She knew the doctor had to fight back, but the extra kicks had been too much. They were just plain cruel.

She wasn't sure what she was going to do, but the little voice in her head demanded justice for Ricky, and she knew she'd get it somehow. Even if that meant writing a letter to the state and risking her employment—and her future—at Pennhurst.

She walked with a heavy step back to Ricky's cell. There was no telling what tomorrow would bring for Ricky, but at least he'd get a good night's sleep tonight. Thanks to her.

Before she entered, an orderly asked, "You need backup in there to give him his shot?"

"No," Christina answered. "I'll be fine."

"He's all yours, but I'll be right here in the hallway."

She opened the door and saw Ricky inside, under the rumpled covers. She had seen this behavior before and was sure he was coping with the situation by using the blankets to hide his emotions, the way a kid does when he knows he's in deep trouble. *Or when he's scared,* she thought.

She shut the door behind her.

"Ricky, you okay?" she asked.

No answer. She sat on the corner of the bed. She could see his wrists poking out from under the cover, restraints locked. She tried again. "Ricky, it's me, Christina. It's okay to be scared. You can talk to me."

"Not scared," he finally said through the blanket. Christina thought he sounded a bit different, but maybe he was putting on a voice?

"Are you hurting?"

"Not anymore."

Not anymore? What did that mean?

"My time's coming up, and there ain't nothing you can do about it," Ricky's voice grumbled.

"Don't say that," Christina protested, pulling back the blanket to see Ricky's pale face staring at her, mouth open. She looked at his eyes, but there was nothing there. He wasn't blinking. His lips were turning blue. A trickle of blood dried in the corner of his mouth. Ricky was gone.

"I told you," the voice groaned. "I told you it's time."

But the voice wasn't coming from Ricky.

Christina bolted up. She stared at Ricky's body—at his face, forever frozen in a tormented gaze. She heard his voice again: "Get me out of here, girl." But again, his mouth was not moving. He was not speaking, yet she heard his voice as clear as day.

Was she going mad? Was Ricky still speaking to her? Had Pennhurst finally corrupted her mind? Was Christina going to find herself in here one day, restrained and drugged at bedtime, a pill in one hand and a vein full of knockout juice in the other? She dropped the syringe, and fluid splattered as it smashed on the floor.

She turned to leave but again heard the voice.

"Get me out of here . . . ," the little voice whispered.

And that was when she saw it: a little hole in the wall—in the same place Ricky would put his ear. The voice sounded like it was coming from *inside the wall.*

Christina held her breath and bent down to look into the hole.

An eye blinked at her.

She shrieked, falling backward onto the floor, but remained focused on the eyes peering out at her. That familiar raspy groan said once more: "Get me out of here."

The wall around the hole began to crumble, like it was being ripped out from the inside. Shaking with fear, Christina watched as the pieces dissolved, revealing the face of a man using the last of his strength to tear a patch of plaster away. He was tangled in the pipes between the walls, like a marionette caught in his own strings.

"Get me out of here. *Lick-et-eeee-split.*"

Christina could tell he was badly emaciated, and barely able to move. He sat perched on the pipes, like a ragged flesh-and-bone ghost, surrounded by dead insects he'd been feeding on to keep his blood pumping. His face was a pale white mess of sagging skin and scar tissue that surrounded his black eyes. He had Pennhurst scrubs on.

But no shoes.

The horror spread across her brain like a storm: *The invisible man who escaped.*

The man from her stories. *Two empty shoes. An invisible man.*

The man they'd said vanished.

He hadn't escaped Pennhurst after all. He had burrowed into the inner workings of the structure and gotten caught in the network of pipes that ran through the asylum's insides. He was too weak to move, but he could talk.

And he was talking to Christina.

The man in the wall.

"Name's Buck," his voice wheezed from the wall.

Buck, Christina realized. This was Ricky's Buck.

The kids were wrong, Christina thought. *If only monsters lived in Pennhurst. That would be much easier to believe than what I'm witnessing right now.*

"I told that boy to go to the light, and he did," Buck said with a grin, his lips curling over his rotting teeth. "He likes being told what to do. Do you?"

Christina's mind kept reeling, filling in the blanks. Buck had been talking to Ricky through the walls. That had to be it. Buck demanded things. Awful things. And Ricky did them.

Ricky had no friends in here other than her. He had no parents. He had no one but Buck. A man who spoke to him and needed him. He needed Ricky to do the violent things he couldn't do to the people who had once locked him away.

All Buck needed was a puppet.

And all Ricky needed was a little voice to guide him.

A hush fell over the store. Nancy stood up to finish her story.

"Christina soon found out who the man in the wall truly was," she said, clicking the flashlight off. There, holding the moment in the dark, she finished: "His name was Harland Buck, and he was believed to be the first patient to successfully escape Pennhurst. Though as we all know now, that wasn't true. He'd made a home for himself there. He'd lived and died there. His story was national news. Christina read all about it from the comfort of her family home in Virginia, where she'd moved back after fainting on the job during that fateful night at Pennhurst Asylum. A night she'd never forget.

"She is no longer nursing. But she's always listening. But is she hearing her little voice? Or someone else's?"

CRASH!

The sudden noise jolted everyone in the store at once. Then there was a long silence.

"What the hell was that?" Robin finally said.

"Holy crap, something TOUCHED me!" Dustin shrieked.

"Henderson, calm down! Stay still!" Steve called, clicking his flashlight on. A chill spread through the store, making the little hairs on the back of their necks stand up. Steve's light-beam shone past the faces in the store, like a searchlight scanning the shadowy grounds of a prison yard during an escape . . . eventually finding Dustin . . .

. . . standing in front of a TAPE RETURN slot . . .

. . . a pile of Family Video tapes at his feet.

Steve picked up the tapes and showed them to the others. "It was someone returning tapes. You're all fine, buncha scaredy-cats."

"I wasn't scared," Mike said.

"Me neither," Lucas added.

Erica pointed at Dustin in the dark. "It was that nerd, right there. He scared himself."

"Sorry, guys," Dustin said, catching his breath. "I've just been on edge lately. Haven't been sleeping well." He took his mini flashlight back from Nancy to make sure nothing else was hiding in the shadows around his feet. "Haven't been sleeping much at all."

"Oh yeah? Up late with Suzie on the radio?" Robin asked,

teasing Dustin about his girlfriend from summer camp.

"No, it's not like that," Dustin said. "I've been going through something intense over the last few weeks. Something that's hard to explain. Something that chills me to the bone."

"Oooooh, do tell!" Max said, intrigued. "I feel a scary story coming on."

Dustin shuddered just thinking about it. But maybe, just maybe, it would help to talk to someone about it. Even if that someone was seven of his closest friends.

Dustin turned the flashlight beam up under his chin and gulped down his fear. "What I'm about tell you . . . ," he said, his voice becoming more and more serious, ". . . is not for the faint of heart. I may just be losing my mind. Or I could actually be at the mercy of dark forces here. Which is it? It's a roll of the dice. That's why I call this . . ."

DO OR 20-SIDED DIE

First off, to truly understand the ramifications of what I'm about to tell you, you need to understand 20-sided die. Most of you know this stuff already, but some here may not. (I won't name names or anything, but you know who you are. Ahem.)

The square dice you play Yahtzee with are not what I'm talking about here. That's kid stuff. The most you can lose in games with square dice is a turn or maybe some fake money with funny colors.

In games like D&D—or any tabletop role-playing game,

for that matter—all that stands between you and certain doom is an icosahedron die. Everyone still with me? Good. Your character has a certain amount of hit points and armor points and other awesome magical stuff. I'll skip ahead on because I feel some of you rolling your eyes at this even though it's super important. The number you roll on the die means everything. A high roll could help you vanquish an enemy or magically heal yourself during battle. A low roll is pretty much a death sentence for you and your party.

The point is: the twenty-sided die determines your chances of survival in any given scenario. **YOUR VERY LIFE DEPENDS ON THE NUMBER YOU ROLL.**

And so, with that PSA out of the way . . .

It all started a few weeks ago.

I found myself riding my bike around, on the other side of the quarry where that corn dog place used to be. It was an overcast day, but there was no rain, just a cool breeze that seemed to push my bike along in an easterly direction. I mentioned the corn dog place. Well, they weren't the only ones to set up shop around here and quickly fold. No businesses on that side of the quarry—the wrong side of the quarry—last very long.

Except for one. A magic shop called Prestidigitation Station.

I had made friends with the owner of the place, an old Italian man named Vivaldi. Despite desperately needing the business to keep the lights on, the old coot never pushed his wares too hard on anyone. Don't get me wrong: he kept the place clean, and was always very welcoming. He loved to turn up the organ music and entertain visitors with sleight of hand stuff or a series of quick and easy illusions. But his magical demonstrations felt genuine, like he was doing it for love of the art form, and not just to make a quick buck off kids with allowance to burn.

"And, presto . . . it's Dustin-o!" Vivaldi would say whenever I entered the shop, ringing that little bell above the door.

"Whaddaya got for me today, Vivaldi?" I'd say back to him, fully knowing he was going to show off his newest gags and tricks regardless of whether I asked. And as he pulled out some Chinese finger cuffs, or disappearing inks for writing secret messages, my eyes would wander to the top shelf of the glass case between us.

And there she was, a treasure fit for any Dungeon Master: an antique twenty-sided die. Now, this was no normal plastic white die. This die had been carved from real jade, which made it glow a hypnotizing shade of green. It looked oh so rad, with the numbers carefully chiseled in a totally metal-looking medieval type-set. Like Bilbo had Sting and Luke had his lightsaber, I just had to have this. *This twenty-sided die of my dreams . . .*

I slam a twenty-dollar bill down on the case. A twenty for my twenty.

"Dustin-o, you know I cannot. We've talked about this," Vivaldi says in that musical tone of voice.

"Forty, then," I say, slapping another twenty down. "That's two birthday checks from my great-aunt. I'm giving you the last two years of my life's earnings for the twenty-sided die. C'mon, I thought we were friends."

"We are! And that is precisely why I cannot sell it to you. This die you seek, she is cursed!"

"C'mon, don't give me that mumbo jumbo. Trust me: I've dealt with worse. I'm not at liberty to say exactly what, but let's just say I'm not afraid of dealing with the paranormal. I have experience."

"I wouldn't wish this kind of trouble on my enemy. So I have to say again, no. No means no."

The little bell rang behind me. Vivaldi shifted his attention to a group of younger kids coming in to see a few illusions and maybe buy some trick gum. He nodded apologetically at me before excusing himself and heading toward the awaiting crowd.

I should've just left.

But like an idiot, I saw my fingers walking my hand across the top of the case, and around the back of it. It was open!

Like the David Copperfield of Hawkins, Vivaldi was in full-on entertainment mode. He had his back turned to me, pulling a pigeon out of his vest to limited applause. The clapping was sparse, but it was just enough noise to conceal the sound of me swiping the twenty-sided die and slapping it into my pocket before anyone else was the wiser. My heart was racing. Was I really doing this?? The pointy edges of the die poked my thigh and snapped me back to reality.

More than the rush, I felt slightly guilty, and decided to do the right thing. I couldn't steal from Vivaldi, so I folded both twenty-dollar bills and carefully left them in the glass case, where the die would normally be. I hoped he'd understand. If not, he was now forty bucks richer, so not a total loss, right?

"TIME OUT!"

Dustin swung the flashlight away from his own face and across the store, eventually landing on Erica. He could see she was sitting forward with one hand on top of the other in a T shape—the international sign for "time out."

"There's no magic shop by the quarry," Erica said, skeptical. "And I should know. I'm there almost every Thursday, shooting fireworks."

"Is that where my firecrackers have been disappearing to?" Lucas asked, shaking his head in disbelief.

Erica held her hand up. "That's not the issue here. The issue is that Dustin is making all this up."

"I *wish* I was making this up," Dustin insisted. "This isn't one of those places with a giant sign out front. It's discreet. You have to know to go in and shop there. I'm actually not surprised you've never heard of it."

"I'll stop in next week, then . . . and see if you're telling the truth."

"You may want to think twice about buying anything from there, especially after you hear the rest of my story."

That evening, the Hellfire Club, my D&D group, had its usual session, and I was planning on my character having a legendary winning streak of epic proportions. I'd slay anything with more than two eyes, lead my party out of any dungeon, and spellcast heaven and earth with my new jade friend in the palm of my hand.

I showed it off to my party as we sat down at the table. Fanfare immediately followed.

"Henderson, rock on!" Doug, my metalhead Ranger said, throwing up the devil horns.

"Is that real jade?!" our Dungeon Master asked, taking a closer look through his specs like a prospector. "How'd you score a choice piece like this?"

"This is the coolest thing I've ever seen!" Vince, our Cleric, said with a grin. "Bro, we can't lose!"

Only I couldn't roll anything above a four. The session was a complete and utter massacre.

"A dark mage has cast Fevered Dreams upon you. It spreads like a rash from your brain onto your flesh," the Dungeon Master announced. "How will you counter?"

"I'll summon Magic Circle," I said, rolling a two. Groans all around from my party at the table.

"A pack of lycans have spotted you," the DM taunted.

"I withdraw and dash into the shadows," I think out loud, rolling the jade die. It stops rolling on the number one.

"The lycans are already upon you. Their vicious jaws are

laced with deadly poison."

"Son of a—"

To add insult to injury (or, let's face it, multiple injuries), my character had lost all weapons, a few pints of blood, and whatever magical healing abilities I had. All I had left was that twenty-sided die. I might as well have ripped up my character sheet and started from scratch.

"Hey, Dusty-Poo," I heard some smart-ass say, imitating Suzie. "Why don't you throw your fancy jade die at the wolves? Maybe they'll feel bad for us and only devour your guts and leave the rest of us alone."

They laughed and I cried. On the inside.

I sat there, helpless, as the lycans devoured my character's entrails like a pack of ravenous piranhas.

My bike ride home that night was the longest bike ride of my life. I kept replaying every awful roll over and over in my head. Those medieval-style numbers—the ones I thought were so cool in the store—now felt like they were mocking me with those 2s and those 4s and that awful, world-ending 1.

Maybe Vivaldi was right; maybe this godforsaken twenty-sided jade die truly was cursed. I dreaded having to face him again after I'd gone behind his back, but what choice did I have? I had to return the die to its rightful owner before my D&D reputation was ruined for good. My mind was made up. I'd sleep off today's disastrous loss and hit Vivaldi's right after school. I'd apologize, return the die, and maybe even get my forty bucks back. It'd all work out. Somehow . . .

To get my mind off things, I tried watching some *Robotech* before bed, but I couldn't concentrate. No matter what position I was in, I couldn't get comfortable. I was hot, then cold. Then hot again. Sweat trickled down the back of my neck. My mind was racing. I felt the die against my leg, even though it was in my backpack, which was all the way across the room. Was Phantom Die a thing?

It had to be, because it was haunting me in a very real way.

It began as a slight tickle, then reared its ugly head: the Itch from Hell.

Around the Phantom Die spot on my leg, right where I'd stashed the twenty-sided die in my pocket that afternoon, a crazy itch now burned like wildfire. The more I scratched and scratched, the farther it spread across my skin. Within minutes, the rash seemed to move up my body and down the length of my arm. I thought I'd put some calamine lotion on it, but my mom said she'd thrown it all out because it had expired. That pink bottle has been sitting in our bathroom forever, and now, of all times, Mom decided to throw it out.

Coincidence? I think not.

Conspiracy? Unlikely.

A curse? *Well . . .*

The aggravating sensation of the Itch from Hell kept me awake as I saw the hours crawl by, tossing and clawing at myself all night like a mutt with fleas. I sat up and looked at my arm in the moonlight. There were hives on it! Gross white bumps like little alien eggs all across my forearm. Did I rub up against some poison oak on my bike ride and just block it out of my memory?

I showed Mom and she freaked out right on cue. Forget Vivaldi's, she wouldn't even let me go to school until I saw the doctor. It could have been my imagination, but the area around the hives looked green.

Almost like a shade of *jade* green.

"I wish I could cast a healing spell in real life," I said. To no one. (Things were bleak. I was talking to myself in a mirror and didn't even stop to cringe at myself.)

The following morning, while Mom went out to get more anti-itch stuff from the pharmacy, I saw my window of opportunity. If I was going to get this possibly contaminated, possibly cursed die out of my life, it had to be now. I bandaged up the rash and biked under a gray sky to the other side of the quarry. Corn dogs didn't even cross my mind. Not this time. Not while that die was still poking me in the thigh, like a little ball covered in daggers.

As the road under my wheels turned to gravel, I began to hear noises. Quiet at first, but becoming louder and more frequent, like the *tip-tap* sound rain makes on rocks moments before it pours. I looked up. There was no rain, not a single drop, but the sound persisted. Something was disturbing the quarry tracks.

Something big.

Something hairy.

I turned to see a blurry shape snap its jaws at me! It nearly took off a chunk of my bike seat. I pedaled faster, screaming. No matter how fast I went, it paced me. The blur barked like a dog, but this was no ordinary dog. It was as tall as my bike tires, possibly taller. Two crystal-blue spheres for eyes that glowed against its matted black fur. Frothing white-yellow spit bubbled in its maw.

The blur snarled and snapped again.

"Go away!" I yelled, but it was no use. The beast became more aggressive. "Screw you, Cujo wannabe!"

Up ahead, I could see the outside of Prestidigitation Station. The safety of Vivaldi's shop was moments away. All I had to do was keep pedaling.

I skidded to a stop and leapt off the bike. I bolted to the door, waiting to hear that familiar bell ring.

But no such sound would be heard.

The door to Prestidigitation Station didn't budge. A Closed sign hung behind the glass for the first time in what felt like years. It was accompanied by a little note from Vivaldi that read *Family emergency. Back tomorrow. Apologize for inconvenience.*

I heard the blur growling behind me. I didn't want to turn

around. I didn't have to—I could see its reflection in the storefront window as it stalked toward me, baring its fangs. Snarling. Snapping. Fitting that I had chosen a magic shop as the place where I would disappear from this planet.

As I turned—

THE BEAST JUMPED UP AT ME!

"Um, what?!" Lucas interrupted.

"Dustin," Mike said. "You've been playing D&D longer than any of us, and the first time you encounter a *real live* lycan, you what—totally forget you can defeat it with something *silver*? You literally jingle around the hallways because of all the quarters in your pockets—"

"Hey! I told you guys, those are for *Dragon's Lair*. You know how expensive that game is!" Dustin explained.

"Exactly!" Mike exclaimed. "Why not throw throw all that silver at the beast?"

"And lose my eleven bucks in quarters? Who's talking crazy now, Mike?! Besides, I threw my bike at it. That's got silver in the spokes . . . I think?"

"News flash, dorks!" Robin interjected. "Quarters are made of copper now. I'm pretty sure I read that somewhere."

As the gang began debating the silver content of quarters and whether or not Dustin's old ten-speed was enough to vanquish the beast, he quickly quieted the room once again: "People, please! Listen up! I was in the middle of a story. Now, as I was saying . . ."

I was knocked back. I shut my eyes, bracing for the unimaginable pain of its jaws tearing my flesh apart.

My arm instinctively came up—the one with the bandage around it—and the beast recoiled. It took me a moment in pure darkness to come to terms with the fact that I was still alive. Still in one piece. I slowly opened my eyes to see the beast for what it was: an abomination that was part animal, part demon. Patches of fur, like a hairy husk, covered the slimy underbody of a monster that walked on all fours, imitating a wolf. It backpedaled slowly, its hind legs bending unnaturally. And yet it never took its glowing eyes off me.

As if it had encountered a force of nature greater than itself.

Now, I'm not saying that that force was me. I'm not the Beastmaster.

I'm saying it was reacting to the rash on my arm, which was now exposed, since the bandage had fallen away in the fray. The beast cowered before the Itchy Rash like it was some diseased *thing* it wanted nothing to do with.

I couldn't believe my eyes.

The die poked me again. And now that I saw I was not about to face certain death, I allowed myself to get angry. "I have been itched, scratched, humiliated, chased, and almost bitten. I refuse to let this thing poke me again," I said, digging into my creased pocket for the twenty-sided die inside.

When I pulled out the jade piece, the beast whimpered.

"Piss off! The both of you!" I screamed, tossing the die.

The beast scrambled away like I was lobbing a bomb with a lit fuse, returning to its blurry form in the distance, before vanishing entirely in the tree line beyond.

And that was when I noticed that . . . the die was still spinning.

"What the hell?" I asked myself.

I got back on my feet and walked slowly . . . *cautiously* . . . toward the jade twenty-sided die as it hummed to a stop amid the black and gray rocks of the Hawkins quarry.

In throwing it, I had just inadvertently rolled a three.

The dice was behaving *as if I was still playing.*

Vivaldi's words echoed in my head: *". . . she is cursed . . . I wouldn't wish this trouble on my enemy. . . ."*

A part of me thought the old man was doing a bit, talking up the cheap jade knockoff to add some mystique to it. But I had encountered nothing but trouble since I swiped it. Maybe this object truly carried some evil, life-wrecking curse. . . .

"The old man was trying to save my life," I realized too late.

And then, yesterday's missteps came flooding back in my memory. I put my character's fate—*my* fate—in the role of this cursed thing. I took my life in the palm of my hands, and this die brought me nothing but true terror in return.

"Fevered dreams . . ." I remembered the Dungeon Master saying. "It spreads like a rash. . . ."

I looked at the very real hives on my arm. A rash. Spreading.

"Lycans are upon you," the Dungeon Master also said, moments before wolves chased my character into a dark cave.

Visions of the blur hit me. The beast. A *lycan* had indeed chased me!

But this was no tabletop game. This was real.

I was living out my every move in D&D! I was doomed.

"Oh crap," I said, realizing I had rolled again. What ominous creature was going to come for me next?

The sky suddenly went dark. Clouds morphed into one enormous blob of black above me.

I ran home like my life depended on it. Because it did.

I ran home, leaving the twenty-sided die behind. And my bike. I left in a panic when I heard the shrieking start.

I ran home with shapes surrounding me, shrieking like banshees over my shoulders. They were shadows that had somehow become solid, living things with faces, hands, and claws. This is what I had rolled in the quarry; this was the fresh hell I had accidentally called down upon myself.

A horde of wraiths.

Evil incarnate.

Their dark spirits surrounded me, making me feel claustrophobic, like the air was suffocating me. Air thick enough to choke on, thick enough to stop my heart.

There, in the void up ahead, I could see my house, with the lights on in the driveway. Mom's car was there, which meant relief, for the Itch no doubt waited inside, along with new topical solutions and pills. But no over-the-counter stuff was going to stop the wraiths that kept circling me. I tried my hardest to run a little faster, but my feet were tired. They seemed to drag. I felt like I could barely lift my legs, as if I was running in quicksand instead of concrete.

Every step got heavier. And heavier. And heavier.

"What's *gooooiiiiiing on*?" I manage to say, the words stretching as if I'm talking in slow-motion.

My hand reaches for the door—it's right there, but I just . . . can't . . . touch it . . . for some reason.

I feel the pinprick on my thigh again.

And I reach into my pocket, and my heart flies into my throat.

The jade twenty-sided die isn't in the parking lot of Vivaldi's. It's in the palm of my hand. It never left me.

It wasn't finished with me yet.

I see my mom—and she looks back at me one last time. She screams bloody murder.

I reach for her, but a dark face swoops in through the doorway like a giant and swallows me whole.

And that's about when I wake up.

"Booooo!" he could hear Steve say while giving him a big, overzealous thumbs-down like you'd give a losing team at a basketball game. "An unoriginal 'it-was-all-a-dream' ending?' Honestly, I expect better from you, Henderson."

"Freddy Krueger called. . . . He wants his ending back," Robin added.

"Told ya!" Erica said, vindicated. "He made it up."

The group took turns ribbing Dustin until he stood up and began digging in his pocket. "Am I making *this* up, jerks?"

Slowly and cautiously, Dustin held out something in his hand. He aimed his flashlight at his palm for all to see.

There it was: the jade die.

This was no illusion. The twenty-sided object was really there, right before their eyes. It was just as Dustin had described it. He looked around and, in a grave voice, said, "I woke up this morning and found this under my pillow."

Erica snuck away from the group to cruise the most forbidden area of the store. Her parents wouldn't even let her peek into the HORROR aisle, let alone browse it. But they weren't here.

She pulled a pocket-sized flashlight from her fanny pack and, like a kid in a candy store, started pulling piles of the scariest-looking tapes off the shelves, pausing every so often to carefully inspect the gross-out artwork on each box. Wishing, hoping, to see the cinematic horrors inside.

"*Evil Dead . . . Poltergeist . . . Friday the Thirteenth?*" she read out loud, her mind suddenly reeling. "Wait. Do you guys have a generator?"

"Are you kidding?" Steve asked. "The bosses are way too cheap for that."

"Dangit. No popcorn, no movies, no power. This place sucks."

Robin tossed her a few Red Vines. "There are worse places you could be during a blackout. Trust me."

"Like where?"

Robin looked at Steve, as if this summoned a taboo subject between them. They shared a knowing look, until Robin finally said, "I mean, we *are* telling scary stories."

"Not this again," Steve protested.

"You can help me tell it."

"Hello?" Lucas piped up. "Tell what?"

"Not what, *where*," Robin corrected him.

Steve joined Robin. She tilted the flashlight and the glow

illuminated his face. Steve paused to check that his friends were listening. He shook his hair to make sure it looked good, then he spoke.

"Some of you might already know this story. Most you probably don't. But all of you know the place. "We're talking about . . ."

LOVERS' LAKE

Today, it's Hawkins' #1 make-out spot for teens.

But wind back the clock ten years and you'll find that Lovers' Lake wasn't the scene for a love story. It was actually the backdrop for a terrifying tale. The kind of spooky story kids will whisper to each other at sleepovers for years to come. It goes like this . . .

Labor Day weekend, 1975. The hair's longer, the air's cleaner, and the road is wide open. A T-Bird comes roaring down the highway, leaving a trail of little paper hats flying behind it in the wind. The people in the car threw those hats like they were graduating, because in a way, they were. They had spent the last nine months interning at Pennhurst Asylum for school credit, and after this weekend, their lives would truly get started. It was a happy time.

Brody, the blond macho man behind the wheel, had accepted a residency at another mental hospital out of state. As had his buddy, Matt, who was anxious to hook up with one of his fellow interns before he had to leave town. They both had designs on Julie, the one girl every staffer at Pennhurst had a crush on. She was as bright as she was beautiful, which meant neither guy stood a chance. And then there was Claire. No one was interested in her in that way, but she was perfectly fine with that. Brody, Matt, and Claire were work friends, not friend friends. And frankly, she didn't want anything to do with any of them after this weekend. She was just along for the ride. She had no family, no local ties to Hawkins. She had her choice of residencies at a few clinics across the country—all very exciting opportunities that any psych student would salivate over—but she didn't want to think about any of that now. Not when there was beer to drink, and fresh lake to swim in.

Claire let her mind wander during the drive, ignoring the conversation to let the road underneath the tires lull her into a state of calm. Before long, that road turned to sand and the T-Bird's engine went quiet. They had arrived. And better yet, they were about to discover that they had Lovers' Lake all to themselves.

"Whoa, what are the odds?" Brody asked the group. "I thought we'd be fist-fighting the townies for parking. This is how you start the weekend off right."

Matt high-fived him. "Damn straight!"

As Julie slinked out of the T-Bird's backseat, the guys were too busy staring at her legs to notice the next odd thing about their new weekend surroundings: there were no houses nearby. Claire had clocked this little oddity the moment they'd driven down the unusually quiet back roads leading to this place.

If something happens to us, there's no one around to help for miles, she thought. *We're all alone out here.*

Claire shuddered.

The others may have asked her to help them unload the ice chests from the trunk, but if they had, she hadn't heard them. Her attention was fixed on yet another strange detail about Lovers' Lake.

There, gently drifting in the middle of the lake, was an old wooden boat. It floated around, making circles, with its oars still poking into the water.

There was no one in the boat.

As if whoever had been rowing it had just vanished. *Poof.*

"Sweet! Free boat!" Matt said, kicking off his flip-flops and heading toward the water.

His reaction baffled Claire. "You don't think that's a little weird?"

"Not really. Boats are things that go in the water, right?"

"You know what I mean—"

"I'm sure the local kids leave it out here," Julie said, trying to keep the tone light. "It's like a raft we can all swim to when we need a place to rest after swimming around."

"Or after skinny-dipping," Brody teased.

"Hold on."

"What?" Steve asked with a smirk that spoke volumes. He knew exactly what.

"No one's skinny-dipping," Robin decreed. She nodded across the counter toward young Erica to clue Steve in to her train of thought. "Let's keep this story PG-13. *Ixnay on the udity-nay.*"

"We've been over this: I took French in high school, not Latin."

Dustin snorted at that. "She's speaking Pig Latin, you dork."

"Yeah, I didn't take that either," Steve said, missing the point.

Robin took the flashlight from him and stepped forward. "You know what? Everyone's clothed at Lovers' Lake. There."

Then, judging by the confused faces of the group, she added: "Not fully clothed, mind you. It's not like they're jumping into the water wearing everything they own. That would be insane. I mean they're all in proper swimsuits. But it's all good clean family fun."

Steve just stared ahead for a moment, as if he had brain freeze. "Great, now all I can picture is a group of nerds wearing parkas and practicing the backstroke. You made me lose my place. Where was I . . . ?"

"You're a real Mark Twain, Steve. You know what? Let me handle it from here," Robin announced. "I take you back to Lovers' Lake for the *real* story."

Brody and Matt ran straight in until they were neck-deep, treading water. The guys whooped and hollered, trying to downplay how cold the lake was, but Claire knew better. Despite the sun beating down on it every day for the past ninety days straight, the temperature of Lovers' Lake wouldn't get above fifty degrees. Hawkins water was funny that way. It was like the winter lived under the surface to chill the townsfolk, even during the warmer months.

And night was falling. What little warmth was coming

from the sun was disappearing by the second.

"You coming?" Julie asked.

"I think I'm gonna stay behind, maybe get a fire started for us," Claire said.

"Don't leave me alone with those two out there. I need backup."

Claire looked over Julie's shoulder and saw the guys waving them in, laughing and yelling like idiots.

Against her better judgment, Claire decided to break free a little and be a "girl's girl" for a change. She kicked off her shoes and followed Julie in, gliding into the water's edge with a smooth dive. The shock hit her almost immediately. Her body stiffened as straight as a board from the icy-cold water. She began kicking and moving her arms, trying her best to get warm. Her old swimmer's instincts kicked in.

Just like riding a bike, she mused. *Underwater.*

Before Pennhurst, before Hawkins, she had been a swimmer in school. She knew your body played tricks on you at this temperature. You'd kick and kick, but it didn't matter how strong your form was; the cold made the water

71

thick enough to slow you way down. You'd work harder, exert more energy, barely move, and tire yourself out. And by that time, it would be too late.

Claire swam harder and shot straight up to the surface. She popped her head above water and took a big gulping breath into her lungs.

She could hear the others in the distance, cheering her on. "Way to go, Claire! Woo-hoo!"

Maybe it was the current, or maybe it was the body's natural need to rest, but all at once the group synced up like a pod of dolphins moving toward a shared destination.

The boat in the middle of the lake.

Despite starting behind them, Claire quickly pulled ahead of the pack and cut through their choppy splashing like a shark. She gained momentum and fell back into her swimmer's rhythm.

Left arm, over. *Breathe in.*

Right arm, over. *Breathe out.*

Always kicking. Never stopping.

Normally, when a swimmer is in a groove like this,

they'll put blinders on so they tune the rest of the world out, focusing on nothing but the finish line. But Claire's tunnel vision was slowly widening, making her aware of the open water around them. It could have been a trick of the eye, but she sensed a shape near her every time her face turned. She initially thought it was a branch on top of the water. Or maybe an oar.

But this branch moved.

Slithered.

Claire tried to ignore it, but the shape seemed to be pacing them, moving in.

A snake, maybe?

The last thing she wanted was to panic the others, but night turned the lake black, and the terrifying possibilities of the unknown made her heart race faster than it was racing already.

Her form got choppy. She too was splish-splashing. And before she could think it over, she found herself calling to the group: "Hurry!"

Breathe in.

"Get to the boat!"

Breathe out.

"Something in the water!"

Panic set in quickly. Between splashes, she could hear the others reacting to her directions.

"What's in the water?" Matt said, freaking out.

"What? What is it?!" Julie yelled.

"Are you trying to scare the crap out of us?" Brody shouted back.

Claire ignored their shouts and paddled her arms harder. She wanted to fill her friends in on the shape, but she needed the last of her lung power to reach the boat.

Instead of lake water, her right hand suddenly gripped solid wood. Claire pulled herself up and rolled over the side of the boat, landing knees-first in gooey slop. She stood up on it, feeling whatever it was squishing between her toes. She blinked the water out of her eyes, her vision adjusting to see her feet covered in algae.

The inside of the boat's hull was also slick with slime.

In the moonlight, it looked like a slimy green and black

coating. Clearly, this boat had been sitting on the water for a while if the algae had built up on it like this, like mold.

Claire shook off her disgust when she heard Brody splashing up onto the boat with her.

"What's your damage, Claire? You almost gave me a heart attack!" Brody told her.

Claire pointed at the water. "Look!"

And finally, Brody too saw the *slithering* branch.

"Aw, hell!" Brody said, kneeling in the algae to get a better center of gravity. If he noticed the slimy algae—and how could he not?—he didn't say. He just held his arms out toward Matt and Julie, who were still paddling a good twenty feet away. "What the hell is that thing?"

"Hurry, guys!" Claire called to them. She squirmed, kneeling next to Brody in the algae and holding her arms out, too.

Matt made it up first, and Brody pulled him over in one smooth motion. Their combined weight rocked the boat, and the three of them swung back and forth like a pendulum on top of the water. They each snapped into action, grabbing the sides and holding firm, trying not to capsize . . .

. . . which meant they weren't reaching for Julie, who desperately could've used the help. Her legs were starting to numb; the water was getting the better of her.

And she could feel something curling around her ankle.

The boat leveled out in time for Claire, Brody, and Matt to see Julie treading water a good ten feet away. Her head bobbed up and down between gargled splashes. Julie tried to scream, but her breath was cut short from the cold and the shock. She felt slimy skin wrapping around her body, pulling her under the current. It felt as if grinding rows of little needles were digging into her shins, gnawing her flesh. She couldn't swim away—she could barely hold her head up.

She finally gasped and gathered enough oxygen . . . to shriek.

Julie's wail cut through the quiet night and sent a shiver up Claire's spine. The others heard her gurgling bubbles, choking, as she got pulled under . . . and didn't resurface.

All that was left of Julie was a little puddle of red that slowly dissolved to nothing.

Brody, who Claire hadn't seen show so much as a shred of

emotion over the last nine months, not even when patients passed away at Pennhurst—patients he tended to every day, mind you—had tears streaking down his face. He was beside himself, traumatized. His shock quickly turned to anger, though, as he began to lash out at Claire and Matt, trying to process what had just happened before their eyes. "You should have reached out to her! We could have saved her! YOU should have saved her, Claire! You were the closest. If we hadn't been saving your ass, Matt, she would still be alive."

He broke down and bawled, falling back onto the algae-covered hull, shaking.

Matt just went quiet, wearing a thousand-yard stare.

Claire kept her eyes on the water. No amount of crying or arguing was going to change the truth: no one could have saved Julie, because she had been the closest to the branch. *Only, that was no branch. It was clearly an eel or a snake of some kind. Maybe a tentacle for something larger, but what?*

Whatever it was, it was still out there—the only thing standing between them and the shore.

Claire waited for Brody to cool off a bit before asking him

to help her row the boat back to shore. It was their only hope. She asked Matt before him, but Matt was unresponsive. He might as well have been a ghost onboard.

Claire and Brody each took an oar and rowed in rhythm, but curiously, though they could make the boat gently spin, they couldn't seem to move out more than a few feet. They would simply circle a bit this way or a bit that way, then float right back to where they'd started. "I think we're caught on something, like tethered underneath the boat," Brody announced. "But I don't think we should dive into the water to find out."

That's the smartest thing you've ever said, Claire thought.

"So . . . what?" Matt said, suddenly breaking his silence. "We can't just sit here all night. We need to get help."

They all sat there, looking at each other for answers, shivering in the dark. An eternity seemed to pass in that silence, during which Matt decided to stop feeling sorry for himself and get brave. "What if we toss the oars?"

"Yeah, sure. We're only sitting in swamp mold while we wait to get eaten, but yeah, things aren't bad enough," Brody scoffed. "Let's ditch the oars. Great idea!"

"They're clearly not doing anything for us if the boat's

caught up in seaweed or whatever. So let's use them to our advantage. We can distract the snake with them. We'll toss them overboard, get its attention, really disturb the water so it comes to investigate. Then we use that distraction to swim to shore. What about it?"

"No way," Brody protested. "Claire might have a shot, but that thing is faster than us. We won't make it, plus we can't see anything down there. I vote we wait until sunrise so we can at least see what's in front of us."

Matt looked at Claire. "Tiebreaker? Deciding vote?"

Claire didn't want to admit it, but Brody was right. The darkness had them at a disadvantage. Matt's plan, while brave, was not smart. "Matt, I know we're in a for long, cold night, but Brody's right."

"Fine, then I'll swim it alone," Matt said, shivering.

"Don't be an idiot," Brody said. "We have a better shot if we stick together."

"You don't get to decide what I do."

As Matt and Brody bickered for seniority, Claire saw bubbles forming around their boat. Something was disturbing the water. Something beneath the surface.

But it wasn't just in the water; it was under their feet.

"What-what-what-what—!" Matt said, startled.

Everyone in the boat suddenly crawled back, balancing on the rim of the boat, trying to pick their feet up off the hull. It was not their imagination: the algae underfoot seemed to be *moving*. It oozed below them, seeping toward the center of the boat and between the planks of the hull. The sludge swirled like water being sucked down a drain. In a matter of moments, the wooden hull was revealed and the water around the boat went still.

They all stayed quiet, holding their breath, trying to understand what they'd just seen. *Algae moving like a puddle before their eyes.* It defied explanation.

Brody looked overboard, seeing his reflection in the watery void.

"If we tell people what we just saw, they'll lock us up in Pennhurst," Brody mused to his reflection.

A wave suddenly crested out of the lake.

Only, it wasn't water.

It was like a net of slimy, wet algae that the lake spit out.

That it spit out.

Before Brody could react, the algae-wave completely covered his head, tightening like a fishing line being reeled in. The organic slop formed around his head, squishing his face until it melted and his eyes popped out. And with one final pull, the indescribable substance sucked Brody's body overboard without so much as a splash. It took him in, thickening the water around him like a gelatinous pit that swallowed him up into pure, goopy blackness.

It was disgusting.

"WAIT!"

"Hold up," Mike said, butting in to the story. "The algae was . . . *alive?*"

"Yep," Robin replied.

"Is it part of the snake thing? Or is it its own thing?"

"That's actually subject to debate," Steve piped up.

"Like hell it is," Robin countered.

"I've heard the story two different ways: the right way, and the wrong way. Now, the right way is that the algae and the slithering tentacle from before are both part of—"

"It's not a tentacle."

"What would you call it, then?"

"It's an eel. Because it's a hybrid animal. It's part eel, part shark, part jellyfish, and the algae are separate organisms that live on it, like those bottom-feeder fish that hook onto whales. That's what makes this so scary: this is a real thing that out's there, right now. People I know have seen it. It's a hybrid—"

"Nope. It's a giant sea creature."

"Don't say 'creature;' don't try to sway the crowd to your side. Say what you really think it is and see if they still buy your story. A sea . . . what? Say the word."

"A sea . . . monster."

Guffaws came from the video store crew. Steve was losing them. "Hear me out," he pleaded over the chorus of voices. "I'm not saying 'sea monster' like Loch Ness or something. I'm not one of those tinfoil hat people. I'm just saying it is common knowledge that something lives in Lovers' Lake.

And it's big. I'm not saying dinosaur, but something that size and from that time. It's been here, in Hawkins, all along, lying dormant on the bottom. Is that so hard to believe, after everything we've seen?"

The video store went quiet once more, each of them knowing all too well what he meant.

Steve took back his flashlight. "No one knows for sure where this monster came from. Only that it's hungry. And it's almost feeding time again. . . ."

Lovers' Lake was getting colder.

Claire and Matt huddled together for warmth on what seemed like borrowed time. Their options for escape were being cut down by the minute. Waiting around all night wasn't going to help them; in fact, it could be a one-way ticket to hypothermia. Trying to outswim it wouldn't work. Even if Matt's distraction idea drew its attention, the oars wouldn't keep it occupied long enough for them to swim to shore. It would know the oars were made of wood. It would know it wasn't prey it could toy with.

It seemed the only thing that would keep the underwater thing occupied was something with a pulse.

And that's when Claire got the idea. She turned and looked at Matt, considering everything she knew about him, which wasn't much. Because they weren't friend friends. They were work friends. Besides his having a psych degree and enjoying leering at Julie, she didn't know anything about him at all. She didn't really know anyone in Hawkins besides these three people.

Now it was down to one.

Claire had no family, nothing tying her here to Hawkins. She was a "stray" who could leave town at a moment's notice without anyone asking after her. Why couldn't she start fresh?

Why couldn't she live?

The idea grew. She'd tell Matt they were going with the first plan—*his plan*—and use the oars to get the thing's attention, swishing the water. Then she'd pull an oar, acting like she was going to toss it over. But really . . . she was going to use it on Matt. She'd knock him on the head and throw him over to feed the *thing*. It would suck his body under and digest him. That would give her enough time to swim back to shore.

It was the only way. And she didn't even have to wait until sunrise. She was tired of being cold. She was tired of hearing her teeth chatter inside her head.

"We should try your idea . . . with the oars," she sputtered.

"Are you sure?" he asked nervously. "What about waiting until the sun comes up?"

"I don't think it matters when we try to leave. Day or night, this thing is here and waiting to feed. We need to act now, before it comes up through the boat again, or we freeze to death in the dark. Your choice."

Matt chose the oar.

Claire even made him help her get it loose. He had no idea what was coming.

He offered to be the one to do the swishing, but she insisted. Claire took the oar in her hands and swished the water to get the creature's attention.

They could see the strange shape bob to the surface. It came toward the boat.

And before Matt could finish saying "throw it over," she

swung the oar and smacked his head so hard, blood streaked across his face in a splash of red. She planted her left foot and went to kick him over with her right, when she slipped!

More algae!

The slop had returned, coating the hull again in its slippery sludge.

Claire tried to get her footing but couldn't. It was too slick. She went heels over head, slipping into the lake. The freezing water stunned her body for a moment, so that she was totally still as she slid completely under and into the dark abyss.

Matt caught himself midfall, his arms instinctively coming out to catch him though his brain was on autopilot from the wound. He didn't fall out of the boat; he just hit the stern. He was laid out like a dead fish, flopping around with shock. The hull algae pooled around him, then slowly curled around his body, covering his stomach, shoulders, and face like a blanket. It squished everything and pulled him down with force, ripping him clean through the hull and snapping the boat in half!

That's when Claire saw it with her own eyes under the water—the algae shrunk around Matt's lifeless body, sealing him in like a cocoon. The algae wasn't algae at all. It was a throbbing appendage on the end of a long, spiny tentacle, part of the *thing* under Lovers' Lake. She could see nothing past that, only blackness. But she could tell it was watching her.

Claire started kicking.

She needed to kick fast and hard if she wanted to have enough of a head start to swim to shore.

She broke through the surface just in time to gulp some much-needed air.

The water coalesced around her, pushing the slithering shape to the surface once again, almost lifting it toward her. Claire was panicking, taking huge breaths and paddling her arms.

Breathe in.

The slithering shape whipped behind her.

Breathe out.

It slithered closer.

Breathe in.

Closer.

Breathe out.

Closer still.

Through the choppy water, Claire could see the shore. Another thirty seconds and she would be free. She shook a vision of Matt's bloody head from her mind and kept kicking. Safety was within reach.

So was Matt's head. Another flash of blood.

No time to think about that! Claire focused on swimming faster and faster.

Her fingers stretched out and soon touched wet earth. She could put her feet down! She felt the squishy earth between her toes—that familiar mucky feeling—as she got her footing, then ran up onto shore and threw herself on the hood of Brody's T-Bird.

She was safe.

She was out of the water.

"I made it!" Claire shouted in defiance at the water. "You didn't get me!"

Air filled her lungs as she looked out onto Lovers' Lake. It looked peaceful, still. When she finally stopped panting, she knew she could breathe easy.

She rubbed feeling into her shoulders, every part of her slowly

warming up, except her feet, where she could still feel the cold, wet sand under her toes. She went to squeegee it off the bottom of her foot when she felt a quick sting. It wasn't sand.

It was the algae!

It ran in a long strand from her foot through the sand on the shore and into the water like a giant seaweed vine.

And before she could scream, it pulled her off the hood of the car and into Lovers' Lake once more. Her face vanished under a froth of bubbles that went from white . . .

. . . to black . . .

. . . to red.

"I'm never going swimming again," Max said as a hush fell over the video store once more.

Dustin and Mike nodded quietly.

"When's the power coming back on?" Erica asked impatiently.

"Trust me, you'll know when it's back," Steve answered. "The store lights will kick on automatically."

Lucas stood at the glass, acting as a lookout. He cupped his hands around his eyes, as if that would help him see through the night better, but it made no difference in a blackout. He sighed. "The streetlights are still out," he observed. "I can't even see stars in the sky. It's dark up there and it's dark down here."

"If only we had the Blood Moon to light our way, right?" Max asked.

No response.

Max sat up from the shadows, trying to get a good look at the faces around her. She couldn't see their expressions from here, but their silence was obvious. They had no idea what she was talking about.

"Tell me you guys have never heard of the Blood Moon," Max said.

"Sounds made up," Mike responded.

"Is that from a movie?" Dustin asked.

"Not everything is from a movie," Lucas told him.

"I knew it," Robin said, hopping off the counter with a

maniacal glee. She sat next to Max on the floor. "You're kinda witchy, aren't you?"

"I'm not," Max admitted. "But some girls in school are." Then she corrected herself. "I mean, were. Some girls in our school *were*."

"So, spill," Erica chimed in, still leaning against the counter. "What's a Blood Moon and what's it have to do with witches and high school girls?"

Max looked at Steve, holding her hands out. "Might as well," she said, nodding for the flashlight. Steve threw it her way.

And with a click, Max was illuminated and ready to explain. "There was a Blood Moon late last year over Hawkins. Now, a red full moon may seem like peanuts compared to what we've all seen, but that's because we don't know how to harness its power. We don't know what it means. We're just looking at it like a moon. Those gothy girls at our school, the ones who call themselves the Daughters of Darkness . . ."

"I remember those girls, the ones who listen to the Cure," Steve recalled.

"Hey, I like the Cure," Nancy shot back, insulted.

"Since when? Oh, right . . . Jonathan."

The back-and-forth melted into an awkward pause.

"As I was saying," Max spoke up, reclaiming the floor. "The Daughters of Darkness go out into the woods during lunar events like that, to do ceremonies and practice blood-magic spells. Real weird stuff. The last time there was a Blood Moon over Hawkins, they went out to do their thing, and they never came back. I heard the true story of what happened that night—the night I'm sure their parents begged them to stay home. But you know how some girls are. . . ."

GIRLS JUST WANT TO HAVE FUN

Despite being inside a lab, during the day, the students of Mr. Klein's third-period Earth sciences class were staring into a lunar eclipse. The image of the full red moon glowed from the overhead projector onto a screen.

"The Super Blood Moon is a lunar rarity that you'll be able to see over Hawkins tonight, and for one night only," Mr. Klein explained. "It's not a 'Total Eclipse of the Heart,' but it is a total eclipse of the moon." He paused for laughter. None came.

Most of the class couldn't care less about their teacher's painful references to radio hits, let alone this talk about some weird moon. But Sam cared. She was laser focused on today's lesson.

Because of the invitation she'd received earlier that morning.

As promised, she'd found it in her locker: a rolled-up scroll. Inside it were a compass, a knife, and a rhyming message carefully scripted in ink:

Like the siren wails and a new night falls,
We band together as the Blood Moon calls.
While they drown in darkness, we are blessed by light.
Join us and be born anew, forever and tonight.
THE DAUGHTERS OF DARKNESS

Sam could barely contain herself. For months, she'd been watching them—a group of four older girls, a mix of juniors and seniors. They wore thick black lipstick, leather jackets, and fishnet fingerless gloves. They avoided pep rallies and PE like the plague. They went everywhere together. They were friends. Sisters. *Witches.*

And now, after a lengthy courting period, they were inviting Sam to join them.

Hearing the heavy footsteps of a hall monitor approaching, Sam hid the knife, the compass, and the scroll in her bag. She peeked at the forbidden objects throughout the morning, getting a rush each time, anticipating the night ahead.

The bell rang, cueing the usual stampede to lunch. But Sam lingered behind. But Sam stayed behind to admire the image of the Blood Moon a few moments longer.

"Mr. Klein, what makes the moon go red?" she asked.

"Oh, it's dust in the atmosphere and refracted light," he replied, a little startled that a student was pausing to ask a question. "In the Bible, it gets a bad rap as a sign of the apocalypse and the end times."

No, no, no, Sam thought. *It's not an ending, it's a beginning.* It heralded perfect alignment of the planets, which acted as a magical gateway of sorts. Perfect for rebirths, renewals, and inducting a newbie like herself into an established coven.

Tonight Sam would join the Daughters of Darkness and find out exactly what *girls like them* did in the woods when no one was watching. She'd heard stories, of course—everyone in school had. But she wasn't sure what to believe. Were they worshipping demons? Or sacrificing goats? Some kids swore up and down that the gothy girls were responsible for all the spooky, unexplainable phenomena around Hawkins as of late: soda cans floating through the air at night. spontaneous fires breaking out near an abandoned cabin in the woods. But one of the Daughters, Becca, had confided in her that none of that was their doing. She assured Sam that the kids who made those claims were burnouts who also told tales of a little girl hiding in the woods who could supposedly move things with her mind.

It all sounds so unreal, Sam thought. *It's like something from a TV show.*

The Daughters practiced elemental spells, Becca told her. Healing. Bindings. Invoking of the spirits. Things the modern witch could use to live her most fulfilling life.

"It sounds more serious than it is," she remembered Becca saying. "We mostly do it just because it's fun. You like fun, don't you?"

Later, in the privacy of her bedroom, Sam underwent a major transformation.

Off came the sweater and dowdy blouse, and on went the leather jacket, fishnet fingerless gloves, ripped pants, and combat boots. Everything in black, of course. In a haze of hair spray, she teased her hair up like Robert Smith, singer of the Cure, and applied so much eyeliner she looked like she could star in an old silent horror movie.

Sam took one last look in the mirror to see herself—*her true self*—for the first time. In this quiet moment, the music coming from her stereo seemed to fade and her mind began to race with doubts. What if this was all some elaborate prank? Or worse, what if the Daughters of Darkness were planning something more sinister for her? Like using her as a human sacrifice?

Isn't that what witches do? Sam thought. She'd seen the stories about "satanic panic" when her parents made her watch *20/20*. But Becca and the other girls weren't like that, right? They liked her . . . didn't they?

Sam looked at her dark reflection. "Well, which is it?" she asked herself. "We just sit here and let Mom use *20/20* to scare us into never leaving the house again? Or do we act brave for once and at least see the Blood Moon?"

Sam's mind, like her face, was made up.

She waited until moonrise and told her parents she was off to a study session with some friends. She chuckled to herself, as neither of those things was actually a lie. Once she was out of the house, she snuck her dad's lantern out of the garage and rode her bike straight to the woods. Becca had told her to find a maple tree with a very particular sign carved into it.

A pentacle.

Sam was to wait for them there.

Using the coordinates and compass the Daughters had enclosed in her invite, Sam found a dark cluster of trees surrounding a large maple tree. The moon's soft red light couldn't penetrate the thick treetops above, so she lit the lantern, throwing a kaleidoscope of light and shadows onto the wilderness around her with a swipe of her wrist. The lantern illuminated something right away. Something unusual.

There, carved in the bark, was the encircled star symbol of the elements.

Sam ran her finger over the grooves of the symbol, channeling a feeling that ran up her finger and down her back. She wanted to chalk it up to being in tune to some sort of naturally magical essence, but her gut told her a different story: unease . . . *fear.*

It was impossible to avoid, standing all alone in the woods after dark. Since she'd arrived and laid her bike on its side, she'd had the gnawing feeling that something else was nearby. Watching her.

An animal, perhaps?

She removed the knife from her bag and held it by the grip in her coat pocket, ready to strike. Just in case. The sound of a whistle soon pierced the silence. Sam spun around to see if she could spot its source.

Something materialized out of thin air right before her eyes.

Impossible, Sam thought, seeing Becca appear from the shadows like magic. She blinked her eyes into focus, realizing that the lanternlight was playing tricks on her. Becca had merely stepped out from behind a tree.

Another girl soon appeared. Then a third and a fourth. They

each carried supplies that ranged from normal (like Pepsi, gas station snacks, and a boom box) to downright bizarre (a live bird in a cage, and a fish in one of those plastic pet shop bags).

"That a knife in your pocket or are you just happy to see us?" Becca laughed. The other girls cackled, too. These were the Daughters of Darkness. Sam hoped that in the flattering light of the Blood Moon, they wouldn't be able to see that she was far out of her comfort zone out here.

She smiled. "I . . . thought I heard something," she told them.

"Well, we are in the woods, honey. There are little critters everywhere," Becca said.

"And in here, too," the girl holding the bird and the fish said. Her name was Tara.

The other two girls were Nikki and Rachel, though it was difficult to tell them apart, as they spent so much time together.

"Welcome to—" Nikki began.

"—our coven," Rachel said, completing her thought.

The Daughters all stood in a line before Sam, holding hands. She didn't know what to do except watch as they looked up at the Blood Moon and chanted an incantation she didn't understand. Soon after, they fell silent, and Becca broke away to take Sam's hand in hers. "Sam, we have divined your interest in us, and have seen inside your heart. You are one of us. The spirits have told us you will make a marvelous addition to our coven, and it is here, under the watchful eye of the Blood Moon, that we will bind your power with ours. Do you accept us in return?"

"Yes," Sam replied, her heart racing.

"Do you invoke the spirit?"

"Yes."

"Then choose your tree and carve the symbol of the Triple Moon into it as a sign of your rebirth."

Sam went to grab the knife in her pocket, but Becca offered her own. It was a larger dagger, with a curvy blade and ornate carvings in the handle. Becca rejoined the other Daughters and waited.

Sam circled each of the smaller maple trees encircling the pentacle tree. Upon closer inspection, she could see that some of them bore carvings of their own, no doubt from the other Daughters' welcome ceremonies in the past. She wanted to be near them, but also wanted to set herself apart in some small way, so she looked for a maple tree of similar height, but one just outside the area.

Just then, as if somehow hearing her intentions, the Blood Moon showed Sam a path through the woods to a shrunken tree that was overshadowed by a mammoth pine nearly twenty feet tall. Though this tiny tree was shielded from the elements, it looked old and a bit withered. The taller pine had soaked up most of the sunlight and rain for itself and left this orphan tree to grow in darkness. The branches had clearly adapted to a life in the shadows, and wore their scars proudly.

Sam felt a kinship with it.

She stepped forward and readied the dagger, hearing the Daughters begin a chant: "*With dagger thus, one with us. With dagger thus, one with us . . .*"

Sam could feel her hand trembling with the weight of the lantern that would light her carving.

"*With dagger thus . . .*"

The stain of red moonlight reflected off the blade.

"*One with us . . .*"

Sam thrust the dagger. But the moment the blade pierced the tiny tree, the bark crumbled away, revealing a hollow inside. Too dark to see anything but rot.

Sam peered into the tree's broken husk, curious. She raised the lantern for a better look.

The black hole inside seemed to be *moving*.

All at once, a cluster of nesting spiders, each one as big as Sam's hand, spilled from the tree. They moved in waves of thirty, forty, maybe more. They were jet-black in color save for one obvious red hourglass shape on all their abdomens, reflecting light the way an animal's eyes do at night.

"Black widows!" Sam screamed, her body going momentarily limp.

Pop! went the lantern as its glass case shattered on the ground. Becca's dagger also slid out of Sam's hand before she got her body to cooperate and pivot into a full-blown sprint, running toward the others. The Daughters saw the incoming swarm and scattered farther into the woods, breaking loose from each other's hands and ducking along separate paths.

The world went so quiet for Sam, all she could hear were her own footsteps on the wet earth. Blood pumping, ears ringing. She nearly slipped when she imagined the little whiskery feeling of their spindly legs creeping along her neckline and down her blouse. She caught herself and got her footing at the last moment. Then she smacked the back of her neck and frisked her arms and legs. Call it instinct. Call it paranoia. Sam believed the spiders were pursuing her because her own senses were telling her that her skin was crawling.

It wasn't.

Sam kept running until her lungs started to burn and her legs could carry her no more. She soon came to a clearing and turned to make sure there were no arachnids on her tail. She saw only grass, branches, and damp, gloomy bushes. Exhausted, she let herself fall to the ground, huffing like she'd run a marathon. She hadn't been this tired in ages. Sweat formed on her forehead and ran down her face, making inky mascara tracks down her cheeks.

Sam centered herself and took a look around. When had the trees thickened around her? The treetops were so thick and the branches so tall, the Blood Moon had become obscured. That meant shadows. Shadows as far as her eyes could see.

Sam had gotten away from the spiders.

But she had also gotten away from the others.

She was officially lost. At night. In the woods.

"This is not fun," she told herself.

Nikki and Rachel were the first to find each other.

"Oh my God," they said in unison.

Nikki took a breath. "I have been looking for you—"

"—forever," Rachel blurted out. "Yeah, same."

The two girls held hands and followed a path, hoping to be reunited with the other Daughters. Fortunately, they soon found their "bread crumbs" in the woods: shreds of wet plastic strips on the ground. Eventually, this odd trail led them to find a dead goldfish where one shouldn't have been:

On land.

There were no ponds or creeks in this area of the woods. The poor creature had clearly been dropped in all the madness after its bag tore.

It wasn't flopping. That time had passed.

Nikki looked at Rachel, and as soon as she said "Tara's going to be so up—" Rachel finished her sentence:

"Upset about her fish. I know! She loves her animals."

They soon discovered prints in the mud nearby. But the distance between the steps made no sense. The stride was much too long to belong to Tara—she was the shortest of the coven. These looked more like animal tracks.

No hooves. No paws. Just big feet with what looked like claws on the end.

Sam backtracked toward the pentacle tree, keeping a watchful eye out for spiders. Thankfully, there were none. The coast was clear—save for two peculiar shapes in the tree line up ahead.

Legs. They were dangling.

She recognized the crazy striped pattern of the stockings. It was Becca!

"Becca!" Sam called, running to see her perched on a thick tree branch high above. She expected some wisecrack to come out of Becca about how she'd gotten up there, or the last time she'd had to climb a tree, but Becca wasn't her usual self.

In fact, she didn't acknowledge Sam at all.

She just sat there, catatonic, with her mouth open.

Completely frozen in terror.

"Becca, are you okay?" Sam asked. "What's wrong? Did you get bitten back there?"

Becca just kept staring off into the dark. "I saw something. Not a spider . . . something bigger."

"What do you mean? Like a coyote?"

"No, this wasn't some animal. It didn't have fur. It had skin. In the moonlight, it looked like slimy skin."

Sam helped Becca down from the tree. "Becca, did we summon something here tonight?"

"We can't," Becca whispered. "We don't have any real powers, not the way people around school think we do. We just come out here to act spooky and have fun."

"Are you having fun?"

"No."

"Me either. I'll tell the whole school on Monday that we did a blood sacrifice and all kinds of creepy stuff if your spooky rep is all you're worried about. No one has to know we're the ones who are scared. Now let's find the others and get the hell out of here."

Elsewhere, away from Sam and Becca, and far from Nikki and Rachel, was an overturned birdcage with a tiny parakeet inside.

Tara's.

The cage rolled back and forth on the ground. The bird's constant flapping was what was making the whole thing rock—strong enough to create motion, but not enough to force the latch open. The parakeet was trapped. It flapped its little heart out, clearly spooked by something nearby.

Something that had the shadow of a man.

But wasn't human.

It stalked forward, effortlessly ripping the cage open with its claws.

The bird's squeak was silenced the moment it rang out. Fangs tore through its delicate feathers, pulverizing its bones with a crunch.

Tara, who loved animals dearly, would have been absolutely gutted by this.

If she had still been alive.

"At least the spiders are gone, right?" Sam said, trying to lighten the mood.

The attempt at humor was lost on Becca.

They walked a circle around the carved trees, waiting for the others to return.

"We come out here almost every weekend," Becca said. "This is the first time I've ever seen black widows, or felt like something was following me. It must be the Blood Moon. What if it brought something with it? Like, something bad?"

"I thought the Blood Moon was a good thing. A gateway," Sam replied.

They stopped walking. In a moment of clarity, Becca stared into Sam's eyes and spoke with the conviction she'd held in her voice earlier. "Something evil could have come through. Something that's been here since long before we showed up."

"Hey!" two voices rang out in the distance.

They turned to find Nikki and Rachel running toward them with open arms, relieved to finally see some familiar faces.

Becca couldn't control herself—she started crying as she hugged the other girls in her coven, grateful to whatever forces had brought them back here safely. Nikki and Rachel hugged Sam as well, including her in the reunion. Her ritual might not have been properly completed, but she was part of this coven now.

"Where's Tara?" Becca asked.

"We were hoping—" Nikki began as Rachel finished with the rest:

"—she was with you."

Nikki handed Becca a shred of wet plastic they'd found on the ground. "We found this—"

"On the ground," Rachel overlapped. "Next to her fish."

Becca and Sam exchanged a knowing look. A shared feeling of dread passed between them.

"We need to get to the police," Sam said. "We're wasting time, when something could be really wrong."

Becca would have agreed if she could answer. Her voice disappeared when she felt her throat tighten at the sight of something watching them.

A shadow in the trees.

"What? What is it?" Sam followed her gaze and saw it too. That gut feeling of unease came rushing back in an instant.

It eyed them in a primal way—like a hunter sizing up its target. It radiated a seething rage and bloodlust that was not lost on the remaining Daughters. They could feel its power. The girls froze, afraid to move so much as an inch while it held their attention.

Then its head opened up like flower petals blooming.

Its fangs were visible in the light of the Blood Moon.

It was some kind of monster.

Without so much as a word, the girls all took off running in one direction, back toward civilization. They could hear it pursuing them. Heavy footsteps clomping in the mud, striding after them with a frightening speed.

Then came its earsplitting shriek.

Sam could hear Becca and the other girls repeating something frantically. A spell of some kind. An invocation of protection. Or some sort of defense, she thought. Whatever it was, it wasn't working. The creature was swiftly gaining on them. She could practically feel its hot breath, wet breath on the back of her neck.

"Whatever happens," Sam said, nearly out of breath. "It was nice to belong, even if it was for just a moment."

Sam tried to keep up with the others but felt her feet suddenly leave the ground.

Something was lifting her by the back of her jacket.

Becca realized they'd lost one of their own. She and the others slowed down, turning to see the creature toss Sam over its shoulder in one motion. "No!" she cried.

"Run!" Sam called back, closing her eyes as the beast crawled toward her, about to pounce, moving in for the kill. She clenched her fists, feeling her fingers tighten around something in her pocket: *the knife*. She clutched the handle and forced the blade through her jacket. The tip pierced the creature's side as it tried to bear down on her. It let out a high-pitched squeal of pain.

That was all Sam needed to flee for safety.

With her heart beating in her throat, she sprinted as fast as her legs could carry her, in the direction of something safe, something *familiar*: the Blood Moon. It was indescribably beautiful. Its muted glow marked the vast darkness above with a giant red dot in the atmosphere, like a beacon back to the real world, as clear as the red marks she'd seen on the black widows. Only, she wasn't scared this time. Instead, the view of the moon brought with it a strange warmth that rushed through her body in waves.

Adrenaline.

Hope.

Sam eventually caught up with the remaining Daughters of Darkness on the side of the road. It was another tearful reunion—each of them sobbing for the loss of their sister Tara. Then came the overwhelming feelings of guilt, and then relief.

Relief that they had somehow survived.

They might have escaped the forest, but the girls knew they weren't out of the woods. Not yet. It was the dead of night, and they were in desperate need of a ride back to town. Away from this doomed place.

Away from the creature that might be lurking in the shadows.

The girls screamed at each car that passed, begging them

to pull over, but the fact of the matter was people in Hawkins were just too scared to pick them up. Gothy girls wandering the street in the middle of the night were a big red flag to most drivers. The Daughters soon resorted to standing in the middle of the road, like a human chain, but that only forced cars to drive around them, honking furiously. Finally, after they hadn't seen a car for what seemed like an eternity, Sam was able to wave down a beaten-up beige minivan that was puttering by. She recognized the vehicle. And the driver.

And somehow seeing past all the tearstained makeup, the driver recognized her.

"Sam?" the kind old woman asked, rolling down her window. "That you?"

"Yes, Mrs. Charlotte," Sam said frantically. "Please help us! We're just trying to get home."

"Of course, hon. All of you, get in!"

Becca, Nikki, and Rachel piled into the back seat. Sam sat up front next to Mrs. Charlotte.

"You girls really shouldn't be out this late. Especially back this way. It's not safe," Mrs. Charlotte said, slowly creeping down the road. "What happened out there tonight? Do your parents know where you are?"

None of the girls answered her, and rather than press the issue, she did the merciful thing and cut the silence by turning on the radio. Madonna soon broke through the static.

Earlier today, Sam would have asked her to change the station, trying on a goth persona that wasn't really her. But after tonight—after all the "fun" of a near-death experience in the woods—she decided that the Daughters of Darkness weren't for her after all.

Maybe she liked Madonna. And maybe she liked wearing pink instead of black. Maybe she liked being "a square." A loner.

Sam rolled down her window to let in some fresh air. She listened to Madonna sing about true love and first kisses, and she felt normal for a brief moment.

Until her eyes noticed a chain-link fence appear from seemingly out of nowhere. It barricaded the dark woods from this section of the road and had ominous rings of barbed wire along the top. Had she been on the other side of this fence all night and not once realized it?

She looked closer at the scene as it unfolded before her at thirty-five miles per hour. There, on the fence surrounding the woods, she noticed a sign. One that clearly warned:

HAWKINS LAB. PRIVATE PROPERTY. STAY AT LEAST 100 YARDS AWAY.

"Wait a sec," Lucas said, racking his brain. "It's been a while since anyone's gone missing that we know. Did you make that story up? I don't remember any gothy chicks at school named Sam. Or Tara."

Max shot him a look. "Oh, been keeping tabs on all the available goth girls at Hawkins High, have we? That what you and your teammates do after practice?"

"No, what? I—I was just . . . ," Lucas stammered, grateful that the lights were out so Max couldn't see him blushing. "Just checking up on *your* story. I'm interested in what *you* have to say!"

Erica swiped the flashlight from Max and shined it back on herself. "Let me get this straight: you guys have been making stuff up all night?" She then swept the light across the other faces in the store. "The witches? The sea monsters? The guy in the wall? None of that ever happened?"

The voices all came rushing out at once. A garbled mess of "It's true!" and "Of course it's real!" and "It happened, just ask so-and-so . . ."

"HEY!" Erica shouted, quieting the group in an instant. She held the flashlight under her chin. "I'm done with make-believe kiddie stories. Time to get an R rating in here. You want to hear something that's one hundred percent absolutely scary, totally messed up, and completely true?"

Erica took their silence as a challenge. "I'll tell you what I heard . . . just don't argue, don't interrupt, and whatever you do . . ."

DON'T BE A PEST

Jerry pretended to be asleep.

He had had a lot of time to practice this—seven months exactly. And in that time, he had gotten his routine down the way an actor learns a role, eventually *becoming* the character. He'd insist he was too tired to watch TV with the family after dinner, brush his teeth, and then wheel himself to bed.

Jerry used a wheelchair.

That wasn't part of the character. That was his real life.

But it hardly slowed him down. In fact, the chair made him quicker. And it helped keep him stealthy during his little performances. He could silently glide in and out of his house at all hours of the night without anyone knowing. But that was *after* he performed his big "sleeping scene." He would roll into his room, hit the lights, and climb into bed. Then he quietly listened for footsteps in the hallway. That was when his performance really began.

Jerry wouldn't clamp his eyes shut too tight. That was a dead giveaway. Doing that is what gets kids caught faking sick. Jerry knew it was all in the eyes. He'd calmly lower his eyelids, relax his face, and remain perfectly still with his mouth slightly open. That was what sold the illusion. Well, that and his breathing. A kid's first instinct would be to snore like a cartoon character. That was a rookie mistake. Jerry knew to take slow, regular deep breaths. To the untrained parental eye, he looked like he was knocked out cold. His mom bought it every time. She'd give him a tiny kiss on the cheek, tuck him in, and shut the door. He looked like a sleeping little angel.

Except he was silently freaking out. Pretending he was scared every moment of the day was another act he'd gotten really good at.

You wouldn't know it by looking at his "sleep face," but Jerry's heart would start to pick up, waiting for the familiar chain of sounds he heard each night. First it was the keys jingling, then the door opening, then that awful van's engine choking to life in the driveway. That was his signal to break character and move into position.

He'd put his glasses on, quietly get into his chair, and wheel himself to the window—a perfect vantage point to see the driveway. A few moments would pass until he saw the outline of a man in a Hazmat suit, leaving his house and unlocking the garage. The man would reappear with a tank of mysterious liquid on his back and strange tools in his hands: wands, sprayers, and discs. After setting the gear aside for a moment, the Hazmat man would drive out in the Bug Van.

Everyone on the block knew the Bug Van. It was an old white panel van with a giant fake roach on top. The vinyl on the side of the door read BUGS-B-GONE! Plumes of exhaust would fan out from the exhaust pipe as the vehicle's squeaky gears woke many a kid from sleep.

The Bug Van lived in Jerry's driveway, because the Bug Man lived in Jerry's house. It was his new stepdad, Charlie, who wore the Hazmat suit and loaded the alien-looking gear into the front seat with him. He was an exterminator.

But who kills bugs at night? Jerry always wondered. *And if he kills the bugs, what's he bringing back in those giant bags each morning? Why does he keep the garage locked? And why does he always smell like death?*

Those questions, along with many others, were what prompted Jerry to start faking sleep. He had been doing it to spy on Charlie for months now, but he was no closer to finding out what his stepdad was *really* up to after dark. And it wasn't like he could just ask him. He didn't have that sort of relationship with Charlie.

Plus, Charlie was kind of scary.

Standing at well over six feet and weighing about three hundred pounds, he was like a moving skyscraper to any twelve-year-old. He had slicked-back hair and wore too much cologne and lots of jewelry, as well as a set of keys that dangled from a silver chain around his neck. He almost never took that off. Add all that up and you got a guy that looked like a comic-book henchman better suited to cracking skulls, not chasing bugs. But in spite of his appearance, Charlie was a nice guy—at least to Jerry's mom, Nadine. They'd met at a trade show in the Hawkins Expo Center. She was there selling pesticides and he was there buying. They hit it off and started dating, and seven excruciating months ago they'd tied the knot while Jerry stewed in the church, wondering why God would let this happen.

Why, God? Jerry thought. *Why did you let my mom marry a killer?*

WAITRESS'S REMAINS FOUND; FAMILY FEARS THE WORST

Jerry shoveled another spoonful of Pac-Man cereal into his mouth, his eyes glued to the horrific story on the front page of the *Hawkins Post*. He hung on every graphic detail: *Mariel Winter, a young waitress, went missing ten days ago. After she didn't show up for work, her car was found in a scrapyard with bloodstains on the back seat—*

Jerry's eyes left the story briefly to scan the table and find the cereal box for a second helping. He poured the fresh multicolored mix out as gracefully as he could with one hand, careful not to make too much noise. He didn't want to wake Charlie—who was less than twenty feet away, sleeping on the couch.

He raised the newspaper once again and read on: . . . *Days later*—meaning that morning—*Hawkins police discovered Winter's severed index finger in an abandoned lot behind the donut shop where she worked. Is this the work of the Hawkins Ripper—*

"I really wish you would stick to reading the funnies," a voice whispered.

A hand came down on the paper, slowly squashing the front page from Jerry's view and flattening it to the tabletop. It was Nadine, Jerry's mom. She still had curlers in her hair.

She took the front page and swapped it out for Ziggy and Garfield. "I don't want you reading gross stuff before school. It's bad enough you watch those horror movies."

"I'm less afraid of those horror movies than of the horrors in this house," Jerry said.

"Keep your voice down," Nadine said in a tense whisper. She nodded toward Charlie as a reminder, before adding: "And what is that supposed to mean?"

"It *means* . . . what does Charlie do every night?"

"Not this again," Nadine said, rolling her eyes. "He works—"

"I know, he's—quote, unquote—'working,' but why does he smell like . . . a dead dog when he comes home?"

"How do you know what a dead dog smells like?"

His mom had him there. "I don't, okay? But, Mom, you have to admit he smells . . . *off.*"

"Those pesticides he uses are made of strong stuff. They make him smell when he comes home, but he's good after a few showers. Now keep your voice down, because I don't want you to wake him up. He works very late to help support this family, and he's self-conscious enough about his bug smell without hearing you bring it up every morning."

She playfully ruffled Jerry's hair and began packing his lunch. "Your friends coming to the barbecue this weekend? I need to know how many so I can make sure we have enough burgers and buns."

"I'll get a head count," Jerry said quietly, wheeling his bowl over to the sink. "I'm sure they all can't wait to try Charlie's bug burgers."

"Enough. They're not made of bugs."

"How do you know?"

"Because that's ridiculous!"

"More ridiculous than an exterminator who works exclusively at night?"

"He can't spray these offices while people are open for business. It's a great strategy, if you think about it."

"Think about it?! Think about this," Jerry said in a loud whisper. He uncrinkled the paper to show his mom the front page. "This lady was working at the donut shop that Charlie was spraying last week. Now she's missing. Coincidence? I think not. The other missing person before this was at the bus station. Wasn't he spraying there too? Mom, I think he's—"

"Enough!" Nadine said, fuming, trying to keep her voice down. "You had better start giving Charlie a real chance around here. Now, stop bugging me about him."

Nadine stormed off.

Jerry grabbed his bag lunch and wheeled himself out of the kitchen, stopping short when he saw Charlie shoot him a look from the couch.

He'd been pretending to be asleep this whole time. He'd heard every word.

After a few more nights of pretending to sleep, and spying before dawn, the day of the cookout arrived. It was a sunny Saturday. Sprinklers blasting. Madonna and Bruce Springsteen playing. The backyard was abuzz with couples and kids of varying ages. The younger ones—Nadine's friends' kids—all crowded around the Bug Van, posing for pictures. It was Charlie's bright idea to have it parked in the driveway with its doors open for a photo op.

As for the Bug Man himself, he was minding the grill and making nice with the neighbors and some of Nadine's coworkers. From far away, he certainly looked the part of Mr. Perfect. The life of the party. This crowd would talk pesticides and bug bombs with him the same way connoisseurs would recommend fine wines to each other.

Ah, a fine 1959 can of Raid, Jerry imagined they'd say, sniffing the can's bouquet. *This will pair nicely with my roach infestation.*

Jerry sat all this out, watching the whole scene with disgust at a safe distance from his bedroom window. His friend Ronnie was there, thumbing through the latest issue of the *Hawkins Post.* Another follow-up story on the missing waitress, but all in the past tense.

"So . . . did you tell your mom yet?" Ronnie asked.

"Tell her what?" Jerry replied.

"About your meeting with Mr. Deere."

"He said he's going to call her on Monday."

"I can't believe you got our guidance counselor involved in this. Is he really gonna call the cops with an anonymous tip on Charlie? Your mom is gonna freak, dude! And so is he!"

"I had to get the cops involved somehow," Jerry said, turning around. "My mom won't believe me. Hell, it took me like six months to finally convince you, and you're my best friend. He's a killer. You know it and I know it."

"It's your word against his. You need more than that. You need proof."

Jerry scanned the driveway again, watching Charlie closely, when he noticed something. Something big.

"I've been staring at the guy all day—I can't believe I didn't realize . . . there's nothing around his neck," Jerry said, thinking out loud.

Ronnie was confused. "Huh?"

"Charlie always wears his garage keys around his neck, on a necklace. They're always jingling on a chain when he walks around. He's not wearing it now! That must mean it's in here somewhere. We have to swipe it and sneak in. If there's evidence, it'll be in there, in his workshop."

Ronnie looked at Jerry nervously. It was one thing to talk about Charlie's supposedly evil deeds, but it was another to actually do something about it. This felt dangerous.

"It's now or never. We have to act before he claims another victim!" Jerry said.

He rolled out of his room, toward the master bedroom at the end of the hall. Ronnie acted as lookout while Jerry quickly glided inside and began opening drawers, searching. His nose was immediately hit with that awful death stench again—the odor was coming from the dirty clothes basket in the corner of the room. He thought of his poor mother having to share a room with that. How did she stand it?

Jerry held his nose with one hand and kept searching with the other. He opened a drawer and lifted a folded stack of Charlie's work shirts, and there it was, hidden on the bottom: a set of keys on the end of a long silver chain. He snapped it up and called out to Ronnie: "Ronnie, I found it! We've got him now!"

Jerry turned and froze—Charlie was somehow standing there, staring him down, a hint of anger in his eyes. He stepped forward, blocking Jerry's way.

"You've got *who* now?" Charlie asked.

"I, uh . . . ," Jerry stammered, panicking. He could see Ronnie in the hallway. She was scared out of her mind. "I was, uhhh . . . we were playing a game. Like a hide-and-seek scavenger hunt thing."

"And it involved sneaking into my room and stealing my keys?"

Jerry could feel his face flush. His whole body quaked with fear. "Not stealing, just playing. I didn't mean anything by it. I'll put them back."

Charlie took a big step forward, forcing Jerry to wheel himself back into the room. He shut the door behind them. Jerry watched Ronnie disappear from view.

Charlie bent down, coming eye level with Jerry. Mr. Perfect wasn't joking now. There was an intensity about him. Jerry could feel his contained rage. And in a hushed tone, Charlie said, "You're becoming quite the *pest*, aren't you?"

Jerry didn't answer. He didn't know how to.

That only made Charlie more furious. "Answer when I talk to you, *Wheels*."

Jerry hadn't heard insults about his chair in a long time. He too could feel his anger rising now, almost competing with Charlie's. "Oh, I've already spoken up, Charlie. I've spoken to my school and they're speaking to the police. Your reign of terror is over. And news flash: you stink! You can't do crap to me. The cops will come and they'll find the bodies."

Charlie shook his head and started to laugh. "The bodies? What bodies?"

"The bodies in our garage. You put them there, you murdering psycho!" Jerry yelled. "I won't let you kill again."

"What's going on?" someone asked, opening the door. It was Nadine.

Charlie suddenly lightened up, turning on a dime into a completely different person. "Jerry thinks I have bodies in the garage. He says he's gonna call the police on me. You should probably lock me up in chains before I do anything bad, hon."

Nadine looked embarrassed. "Jerry, please don't—"

"Mom, you have to believe me! He's the Hawkins Ripper. It's him! I swear!" Jerry said, showing her the keys. "Just take these keys, open his garage, and you'll see. You'll find the bodies."

Nadine quietly stepped forward and took the keys from Jerry. "I am so sick of this. We're going to settle things between you two once and for all."

Jerry rejoined Ronnie in the hallway, following Nadine outside. As they entered the yard, it was clear that the party had stopped. No more music. No more laughing. The mood was heavy with that awkward air after a fight erupts or someone says the wrong thing. There were just rows and rows of neighbors, and colleagues, and other kids watching Nadine push her way through the crowd, all eyes on what was about to unfold.

Charlie finally emerged from the house just as Nadine unlocked the master lock on the garage. Jerry gripped Ronnie's arm in anticipation, simultaneously excited and terrified to see what hell awaited them on the other side of the garage door.

Sunlight rushed into the garage all at once. Wheeling up next to his mom, Jerry felt his heart sink when he saw that there was nothing there but tools and boxes. Charlie's bug gear was laid out on a tarp on the floor, as if it were on display. Truly, nothing hidden. The wands and sprayers and bug bombs just lying there. But that was all that could be classified as "different" in this sprawl of standard suburban crap. It was totally and completely innocent.

"Where are the bodies?" he heard Charlie say from the crowd behind him.

Soon Charlie found his way to Nadine in the garage and addressed the partygoers. "My stepson, Jerry, said he thought he saw bodies in here. He thinks I'm a serial killer. Boy's been watching horror movies and reading monster magazines with Freddy Krueger inside, but I'm the scary one somehow. He's been telling everybody at his school all these stories about me, thinks I'm gonna murder him."

Jerry looked around, cringing with embarrassment. He could feel everyone's eyes on him, judging him.

"Well, are you gonna do him in?" asked an elderly neighbor. "You a dangerous man, Charles?"

And without missing a beat, Charlie turned into Mr. Perfect again with a big grin: "Only if you got more than two legs."

The crowd laughed.

It was brutal.

Nadine pulled the garage door shut and folded her arms at Jerry. In her sternest mom tone, she said, "You owe Charlie an apology."

The following day, Jerry apologized.

He didn't bring up the scary confrontation in the bedroom, or how Charlie had tried to intimidate him. It would have been no use. Not when he'd been made such a fool of, in front of everyone he knew within a twelve-block radius. Thanks to Ronnie, Jerry's classmates got wind of what had happened, which meant a version of the events made its way through the school like a game of telephone, eventually reaching the faculty, the principal, and yes, even the school guidance counselor, Mr. Deere. The same man Jerry had confided in from the beginning. Jerry considered Deere a true ally to his cause.

Mr. Deere now thought Jerry was a big fat liar.

No calls were made to the Hawkins police about Charlie.

Jerry had cried wolf, and no one was answering. The whole world had pushed him aside. At least, that was how it felt. Especially over the next few days, when his mom dropped a bombshell on him.

"I'm going to Cincinnati for a business trip," Nadine said, packing her things. "I'll be back Sunday."

Jerry sat in his chair, in the hallway. Stunned. "Sunday?! But that's four days of . . . of . . ."

"Of just you and Charlie? I know. It'll be the perfect opportunity for you boys to get to know each other and get along without your mom in the way. I think some man-to-man time will actually do you some good. Now hand me that curling iron."

Jerry robotically helped his mom pack without further protest. She might have shared some work gossip or told him how to heat up leftovers if he was alone for dinner, but if she did, he didn't hear any of it. He couldn't concentrate. His vision went blurry. The room seemed to spin. *Forget pretending to sleep,* Jerry thought. *I'm never sleeping again. Not as long as it's just me and Charlie under this roof.*

It was cold that night.

The exhaust from the idling Bug Van plumed out in puffs of visible steam. Streaks of moonlight illuminated a familiar figure in the haze—a man in a Hazmat suit.

Jerry secretly watched all this from his window, like he had a hundred times before. But tonight would be different. He'd strike while Charlie was out on the job, before he'd have a chance to clean up the garage or hide whatever was truly inside those giant bags Jerry had seen him drag back along the concrete.

I know you've got something in there, Jerry thought. *You may have fooled everyone else, but you're not fooling me.*

Jerry wouldn't even need to trouble himself with lifting Charlie's key. *I'm going for broke,* he thought, planning to hammer the lock off. He'd seen a car thief do it on an episode of *The A-Team* and realized there was a whole world of creative ways to open doors that didn't want to be opened. Earlier, when he got home from school, he'd dug through the junk drawer in the kitchen, and there it was, under rubber bands and notepads and knick-knacks: an old, dusty hammer his mom kept handy for hanging picture frames around the house.

The sound of van doors slamming snapped Jerry back to attention. He watched Charlie get behind the wheel of the Bug Van and disappear into the night. Jerry took a deep breath and waited ten *long* minutes after he'd seen the van's big fake roach shrink into the distance.

The coast was clear. The time was now.

Jerry gathered the hammer and a flashlight and wheeled himself outside. Up the driveway, waiting to be plucked like a cherry in a tree, was the lock on the garage door.

Charlie's "workshop."

Jerry removed the hammer from the back sleeve of his chair and nervously raised it. His heart was racing. Puffs of his warm breath fogged up his glasses. He was about to cross a line, and he knew it. The punishment would be severe if he got caught, but it would be worth it. Especially if he could save a life.

Or at least prove he'd been right about Charlie all along.

The garage had to be explored, no matter what was waiting there for him.

Jerry swung the hammer down.

The smack of steel on steel echoed through the dark neighborhood. He had to hit it two more times before the lock shattered open, hitting the driveway in pieces.

The garage door rumbled like thunder as Jerry opened it.

He flicked the flashlight on. It sounded like something skittered away into the shadows to avoid the beam of prying light. Jerry wheeled himself in, seeing the garage look as clean as it had at the cookout. Nothing but a bare, shiny floor, and some tools and used tanks set out on a tarp off to the side. He aimed the flashlight at the back wall and saw nothing but big square sheets of wood.

Jerry could feel his jaw tightening.

Was Charlie really just a nice guy who had absolutely *nothing* to hide? Had Jerry made this whole thing up out of jealousy over his mom marrying a new guy? Where were the blood-soaked sheets? The bodies? The rack of torture tools?

"Where's the evidence?" Jerry said out loud, talking to himself.

He sighed, while turning around to wheel himself back to the darkened house.

And then it happened. The skittering noise he'd heard earlier. It skittered again. The sound of little mouse feet scratching against plastic. Did the Bug Man have a rat problem? *That would be hilarious*, Jerry thought.

He turned back around and wheeled himself toward the sound. It seemed to be coming from behind the propped-up sheets of wood. Jerry balanced the flashlight between his teeth, using his hands to push the wood aside.

There was a door.

Jerry nearly broke a tooth biting down on the flashlight handle. He was looking at a secret door hidden in the back wall of the garage. The moment it slid open, he was hit with that *Charlie smell*. His mom had said the scent came from compounds in the pesticides. But Jerry thought it stung his nostrils worse than any chemical could.

It smelled like something had *died*.

Jerry wheeled himself through the entrance, ducking under something that almost smacked him in the face. He aimed the flashlight at it, expecting to see a cobweb. Instead, he saw a glint of steel bouncing back at him.

It was a pull chain for a lightbulb.

He reached up and gave it a tug. The lightbulb glowed, revealing the small secret room around him.

And the pile of bones in the corner.

Jerry went to scream, but all that came out was a series of panicked noises, choked off in the back of his throat. He was looking at a disturbing shrine of sorts—one that appeared to be moving because of all the rats crawling around it, gnawing at the bones. The furry vermin skittered against a strange plastic surface underneath them. Pinned to the wall above this haunting scene, like a trophy on display, was a tiny plastic rectangle. It was maroon with white markings.

A name tag.

Jerry wheeled closer to get a better look at it. It read MARIEL.

Mariel? Jerry's heart felt like it had stopped beating. "The waitress from the news? The waitress who's been missing!"

Mariel Winter was supposed to exist only in the headlines of a morning newspaper, not propped up behind Jerry's house as rat food. He fought through the tears, getting his head straight. This was the evidence he needed to finally bring Charlie to justice. He swallowed his fear and began trying to pull the name tag down, but it was no use. It wasn't simply pinned on the wall like he'd thought. It seemed to be stuck there.

No, not just stuck.

Glued.

So did some of the rats. They seemed to be literally glued to the floor. He watched them try to scratch and bite their way to freedom, but it was no use. It was as if whatever was covering the floor had sealed their bodies to it permanently, leaving them to squeak in agony as they tried to break free.

Jerry wanted to flee, to get to a phone and call the police, but he couldn't turn his wheels. He couldn't even get his chair to roll. His tires were stuck to the same sticky substance. It seemed to cover the entire area. The walls. The ceilings.

The floor.

Jerry's flashlight illuminated a trail of terror that led from the bones to a length of dead insects that had had the unfortunate luck to fly in and get trapped against the industrial-strength glue panels. Jerry's pulse pounded as the horrific truth began to set in. This wasn't a workshop. This was a giant glue trap—a life-size roach motel, where people checked in but they didn't check out.

Charlie didn't exterminate bugs; he'd been exterminating *people* like bugs.

Quaking with fear, Jerry flung himself from his chair, determined to crawl to safety if he had to. But once he hit the floor, his clothes and hands immediately stuck to the surface. He screamed as he tried to peel his bare hand away from the sticky coating. It felt like he was going to tear the skin right off his palm. He couldn't bear the pain. He couldn't break free, let alone crawl.

"Help!" Jerry's screams echoed, bouncing off the walls. **"HELP! . . . HELP! . . . HELP! . . . HELP! . . ."**

"Looks like someone's in a *sticky* situation," he heard a familiar voice boom from behind him.

Jerry craned his neck, seeing a large, imposing figure step through the doorway, covered head to toe in a plastic Hazmat suit. He sobbed. "What are you going to do to me?!"

Charlie lifted a spray wand, aiming its nozzle at Jerry's face. "This is what you get . . . for being such a little *pest.*"

"Hold it right there," shouted another voice from the dark.

Charlie froze.

Jerry saw a flashlight beam come shining through from the doorway. He'd know that voice anywhere. It was Ronnie!

"The police are on their way right now, and my parents know I'm over here, so if anything happens to me or Jerry . . . ," she said threateningly, staring Charlie down.

Charlie dropped the spray wand and carefully backstepped toward the wall.

"Jerry, you okay back there?" Ronnie asked, keeping her eyes leveled on the killer.

"I'm stuck!" he cried, relieved that the nightmare was over before it could get any worse. As police sirens wailed in the distance, Charlie suddenly threw himself at the wall, forcing his way out of the workshop through a loosened panel of siding. It came undone with a nails-on-chalkboard *screech*.

And just like that, the Bug Man ran off into the night, scurrying into the shadows like a cockroach.

"Careful, watch your step," Jerry told Ronnie, pointing out the sticky glue panels on the floor. He looked at her, his mind reeling. "How did you know to—?"

"I've been keeping watch on you since the party," she

explained. "I think because, deep down, I knew something was wrong."

She carefully climbed onto his wheelchair to avoid the floor and stayed with him until the police got there. "My mom called your mom," she told him, trying to calm him down as best she could. "She's on her way home. She knows everything now, Jerry. We all do."

Jerry exhaled. The weight of the last few months was finally off his shoulders.

Seeing the familiar red and blue lights flashing should have been enough to vanquish his fears. But he couldn't see them. Only the jagged hole in the side of the workshop they were flashing through.

That hole brought with it a feeling that would *bug* Jerry for the rest of his days.

The feeling that Charlie was still out there.

Somewhere.

"And that, my friends, is my why Jerry Loomis never returned to Hawkins Middle," Erica said in a grave tone. "Because the Bug Man finally caught up with him."

She clicked the flashlight off and let the spooky silence fill the room.

"Is that . . . true?" Robin asked, aghast.

"Bull!" Lucas said, reaching for the flashlight. Erica tried to keep it, but he wrestled it out of her grip.

"Is not!" Erica protested.

"Is too!" Lucas argued. "That Loomis kid in the wheelchair moved away because his mom got transferred to a new job. I know because I was there when she told our mom the news at their *going-away* party."

Erica tried to get the flashlight back. "Isn't every party a *going-away* party if it happens right before you get murdered?"

Lucas took it upon himself to set the story straight. "Erica's also obsessed with the roach motel. Dead giveaway. She just likes quoting the commercial: '*Roaches check in, but they don't check out.*'"

"But the missing waitress," Nancy said, remembering.

"That happened. I read about that in the *Hawkins Post*."

"Yeah, so did she," Lucas told her. "Don't let her BS you."

"You're such a nerd," Erica said, finally giving up on the flashlight.

"See what I have to deal with?" Lucas said. "The perks of being a big brother."

Lucas switched the flashlight back on.

"It actually reminds me of a story my dad used to tell me when I was little. It was about two brothers, and . . ."

TWO LUNCHES

Two of everything.

That was what Troy's little brother Danny had been asking for, for the past few days. Two sandwiches, two apples, two cookies.

"Two lunches," Danny would say.

Normally, Troy would tell Danny to buzz off and then go joyriding around town with his friends. Maybe sneak a cigarette. Maybe scope out the girls at the public pool. But not this summer. Danny was still too young to stay on his own, and there wasn't extra money to pay a babysitter, not since Dad left and Mom was forced to take double shifts down at the diner just to make ends meet for her and her two boys.

That left Troy in charge.

His duties consisted of minding Danny. And from morning until night, that was what he did, making sure Danny didn't accidentally kill himself jumping off the roof or acting like a little weirdo in the backyard, and of course, keeping him well fed.

Danny's a growing boy. That was how Mom would explain away Danny asking for two lunches instead of one. But Troy had a funny feeling about the whole situation. For one thing, he never actually saw Danny eat the food. He'd hand his little brother two separate bag lunches—per his specific instructions: *two separate bags, please*—and then watch him take it all to the creek not far from their house. For all he knew, Danny could be tossing the lunches in the creek, or feeding Mom's hard-earned groceries to the ducks.

Maybe, Troy thought. *Or maybe I should just be happy*

that the scrawny little dork is finally asking for food instead of playing with it. Danny was small for his age—very short and maybe sixty pounds soaking wet.

So is he eating two lunches? Troy wondered. *Or is he feeding one of his scrawny little friends? Pshhh, yeah, right. He doesn't have any friends.*

One day, just out of curiosity, Troy asked Danny if he could tag along and have lunch with him. "I'd love that, but . . . you're not invited," Danny told him. Then he scooped up both lunches and flew out the back door before Troy could hit him with any follow-up questions. "See you after lunch!"

"I'm not invited?" Troy said out loud, a bit baffled by the phrasing.

Troy was about to say *to hell with this* and just follow Danny, when the phone rang.

He snapped up the receiver and was instantly hit by a commotion on the other end. "Troy? Hello? Can you hear me?" he heard his mother yelling. It sounded like she was at a parade or something. A cacophony competed with her voice, forcing Troy to hold the phone an inch or so away from his ear.

Troy spoke up over the noise. "Mom? That you? Why's it so loud? What's going on—?"

A few miles away from the tranquility of Troy and Danny's house, a stressful scene was unfolding. Cars were backed up for a mile or so. Angry drivers honked their horns, as if that would help move the traffic jam at all. Hawkins police had set up a roadblock and were out in force, not allowing anyone to reach the major highway. In fact, officers were telling drivers to turn around and go home immediately.

And there was Troy's mom, on the side of the road, at a pay phone, yelling over the horns and sirens and road rage swears.

"I'm coming home early," she shouted into the receiver. "I just want to make sure you and Danny keep your butts inside."

Troy looked at the back screen door as she said that. It was still swinging back and forth from when Danny had taken off for his daily double lunch. "Why?" he asked.

"There's a maniac on the loose," she replied. "All the roads are blocked. The cops aren't messing around—they want to find this guy before he flees town. Or worse."

"A *maniac*? Mom, calm down. Explain yourself."

She proceeded to tell Troy what the officers had told her. An inmate—*a patient*—had escaped Pennhurst Asylum, and he was off his meds. The hospital had known about his disappearance for a few days but didn't think to report it until they could be sure he wasn't just hiding on the grounds somewhere. They gave his name and a description: Jimmy Ray Cutts, also known as the Backyard Terror. He was tall, standing about seven feet, and had a bright white shock of hair that stood straight up on his head. He liked to collect victims the way some people collect stamps, so he was to be considered *extremely dangerous.*

The police got involved when an old woman called in, claiming to have seen a man that fit this exact description trying to eat her cat.

"He is a dangerous *lunatic*," Troy heard his mom say, her

voice cracking from speaking so loud. "That's the word they used. So I'm coming straight home and I want you to keep Danny inside today."

She hung up, presumably racing back to her car and cursing the heavens that she was losing a shift at her job. While all Troy could do, a few miles away, was start to panic.

He could no longer hear the dial tone. Just the sound of his own heartbeat, pounding. Danny had already been gone ten minutes, maybe longer.

Maybe it was already too late.

"I know where this is headed."

Erica broke the silence. She clicked her mini flashlight on, aiming it up at her chin, so Lucas could plainly see the look of disapproval on her face.

"Isn't it obvious?" she said with a smirk. "Lucas is making up a story to try to scare me into being more responsible.

Look, if Mom can't scare me into cleaning my room, neither will this made-up backyard boogeyman."

Lucas smiled. "Tough talk for somebody who still sleeps with a night-light."

"How many times do I have to tell you? Glow Worm is a stuffed animal *who just so happens* to be a night-light. It's not my fault he's built that way."

"So you're not scared of the dark?"

"Nope."

"At all?"

"Heck no."

Lucas smiled again, the wheels turning. "Then you won't mind turning off your flashlight and listening to the rest of the story."

Dustin patted Lucas on the back. "Smooth move, dude."

"Don't encourage him, nerd," Erica said. "This is a family discussion."

She clicked her flashlight off. All eyes were back on Lucas.

"Now, where was I?" Lucas paused, thinking. "Oh, right . . ."

Troy had to find his brother.

He threw his sneakers on and sprinted out the door, heading for the creek. He ran past the trees and down the muddy path that led deep into the woods. The gold and auburn leaves of fall crunched under his soles as he tried not to think of his little scrawny brother lying in a ditch somewhere.

Mom's frantic words ran through his mind: *Tall. Bright white shock of hair.*

Troy shuddered as he scanned the area on his run. No sign of another living soul out here. He couldn't even hear birds chirping. A quiet, eerie air hung over the woods that made the world he knew unrecognizable, almost *unforgiving.*

"Danny!" he called. But there was no response. Not even an echo. "Danny, damn it! Answer me, it's your brother!"

Finally, the sound of running water. Troy was nearing the stream.

He tore through the brush, waving the branches clear from his face, until finally . . . he was standing at the edge of the creek. He gulped air, his heart sinking fast.

There was no sign of Danny.

"Danny!" Troy shouted as loud as he could. He searched the area, looking for anything out of the ordinary. "Danny!"

The hairs on the back of Troy's neck stood up. Across the creek, on the other side, something caught his eye: flecks of something peeking out from underneath a layer of yellow fallen leaves. Something bright blue.

Something that shouldn't be here in the woods.

Troy hopped over the narrow stream and ran, never taking his eyes off that spot of blue. A gust burst through, moving some of the leaves with it, revealing more of the strange blue surface as Troy got closer. Whatever the blue thing was, it was tall, and appeared strong enough to stand up on its own but light enough to sway in whatever direction the wind was blowing.

Troy slowed down, stepping softly toward it. He couldn't believe his eyes.

It was a tent.

Troy froze. He didn't want to imagine what he'd find inside.

157

It took all his courage to take a step forward. And another. Then another.

Until the zipper on the front flap of the tent was within reach.

He reached down for a stone near his shoe, picking it up in the event he needed to defend himself. The stone was heavy enough to crack a man's skull if it was thrown with enough force. Troy wasn't sure he had the strength at this moment, but if it came to a choice between smashing a madman and saving his little brother, he hoped he would be strong enough to get the job done.

Troy charged inside, raising the stone above his head.

But there was no one to strike.

The tent was vacant, but not empty. Along with leaves and a thin layer of dirt, crumpled balls of paper lined the floor. Troy unfurled one, recognizing the texture between his fingers immediately: it was once a paper lunch bag.

These are our bags, he thought, his heart racing. The place was filled with them. Along with remnants of lunches past. Torn bread crusts, cookie crumbs, and old apple cores turned green from days of rot.

Two lunches, Troy realized, angry with himself. *Why didn't I follow you the moment something felt off*? In a spike of rage, he kicked the bags out of his way and screamed until the veins popped out from his forehead.

In the corner, bunched together to form a makeshift pillow, was a smelly pile of pale blue clothes. Troy picked them up for a closer look, a strong scent of body odor wafting up. Someone had sweated in these, lived in these, and camped in these. Someone who didn't bother to bathe. Or didn't have the chance. The clothes looked like pull-on uniform shirts, but they were light and airy like hospital scrubs. Printed on the back, where the shoulder blades would be, was a word that made Troy go as white as a sheet:

PENNHURST

As he stood there fearing the worst, the wind picked up again.

Troy looked out at the leaves spinning, a vortex of thoughts turning in his head. *Maybe Danny took the long way back and we just missed each other. Yeah, that's it. Maybe he's hiding, playing a trick on me?* Danny was quirky that way. All kids his age were. This could be his idea of a joke. *Ha ha, I set up a random tent here and thought it'd freak you out,* he could say, giggling in that Danny snort. *Gotcha!*

God, please let this be a joke, Troy thought. *Please let him be back at home, sipping chocolate milk and hiding behind the couch, waiting to jump out and scare me. Wouldn't that be something? Danny sitting at home, just fine. And me, still scared. I'll make all the lunches he wants if it makes him happy and he's alive and well. I'd even let him scare me a hundred times a day, every day, if that's what it took. I'd live in fear. As long as I was living with Danny.*

Please don't let him be dead in a ditch somewhere.

Troy blinked the thoughts away, and the tears. He'd be the one dead in a ditch if his mom found out he'd let Danny leave the house when she told him not to. He dropped the stone and tore his way out of the tent, knocking it down in the process.

Though his legs felt like rubber and his lungs burned, Troy didn't stop running until he'd made it back home. As he got closer, he could see that the paved driveway next to the house was empty. He'd beaten his mom home! Maybe Danny had beaten *him* home.

Troy locked the screen door behind him (just in case) and ran into the living room, gasping. "Danny!" he yelled over and over. No answer. He searched the bathrooms, his heart skipping a beat each time he threw back the shower curtains. There could be anyone hiding behind them.

There wasn't.

"Danny!"

Troy searched Danny's room, looking under his bed and in his closet—all the places Danny might hide. He investigated their mom's room and looked under the pile of dirty laundry in the basket. He peeked behind the couch, opened every cabinet in the kitchen, and threw lights on in every closet.

Danny was nowhere to be found.

"He's really gone," Troy said out loud.

Just then, there was a tapping at the door. Light at first, but then building to a slow, steady knock. *Knock.*

Knock. Knock.

Knock. Knock. Knock.

Troy breathed a sigh of relief. Danny.

Knock. Knock. Knock.

Knock. Knock. Knock.

He went to the door and looked through the peephole. There was no one there.

Or whoever had knocked was hiding.

This could be a trap, Troy thought. *Or it could be my imagination.*

On the next knock, in a moment of bravery, he flung the door open . . . only to find Danny standing there. Too short to be seen through the peephole.

"Oh my God! Danny!" Troy shouted. "Get inside now!"

"Why are you mad—?" Danny asked before his brother pulled him over the threshold.

Troy locked the door and immediately began scanning his little brother for cuts, or bruises, or worse. The kid was fine—in the exact same condition he'd left the house in.

"What's going on?" Danny asked, oblivious.

Troy took a deep breath before his anger took hold. He didn't mean to sound like a responsible adult, but a stern voice of reason suddenly came out of his mouth. "What's going on is that you're off in the woods feeding lunch to deranged lunatics! What happened to *don't talk to strangers*, huh?"

"Jimmy's my friend."

"He's NOT your friend. Now go and make sure all your windows upstairs are locked. In fact, check all the windows."

"Are we in danger?"

"We might be if you don't hurry it up. Now do as I say!"

As he watched Danny race upstairs, Troy shouted, "Wait till Mom hears about this. You're gonna be in so much trouble!"

As Troy double-checked the front and back doors, he heard Danny call him from upstairs. "Uhhh, Troy . . . ?"

"What?" Troy called back.

"Is Mom here?"

Troy paused, trying to understand the question. *"Wait, what?"*

"Is . . . Mom . . . here?" Danny called.

"No. Why?"

Troy looked to the top of the stairs, where he saw Danny waiting, as white as a sheet.

"She's on her way home now, but . . ." Troy said, trailing off when he saw Danny point to the ceiling. Toward a creaking noise coming from just above his head.

The attic.

Someone was moving up there.

But it wasn't their mom.

Frightened silence filled the video store. The dread in the air was palpable.

"So . . . who was in the attic?" Steve asked.

Dustin shook his head. "Isn't it obvious? It was the escaped mental patient!"

"I never said that," Lucas said, shifting in his seat. "It could have been anyone up there."

"So . . . who else would it have been?" Robin chimed in.

Lucas thought about that for a moment. "Well, I'm not sure, I never heard the rest of the story."

This drew instant jeers from the group.

"What kinda ending is that?!" Erica demanded, throwing red licorice at her brother.

"Total copout!" Max added.

"That was worse than Dustin's dream ending," Mike opined.

"Hey—" Dustin said, slightly insulted. Until everyone began to laugh. At which point, he became more insulted.

A sudden creaking noise brought the laughter to a dead stop. After a pause, they heard the noise again.

Creeeaaaaak.

Everyone looked up, their hearts in their throats.

"The store doesn't have an attic, right?" Nancy asked.

A knocking on the glass startled everyone in the store. Lucas clicked off the flashlight and instinctively held his breath, like he was trying to hide from whatever was making that noise. The others followed his lead, whether they realized it or not. No one made a peep. They all sat listening to the quiet, waiting with anticipation, hoping another knock wouldn't come—

Knock.

KNOCK.

KNOCK!

No one so much as breathed. Steve and Dustin ducked behind the counter with Robin. Erica and Max hid behind Lucas. Nancy crouched down, pulling her sweater up over her eyes.

And there was Mike—too frozen with fear to get off the floor.

Until he burst out laughing.

"It was me, guys," Mike said, raising his fist in the air and demonstrating the exact same knock on the glass.

Knock. KNOCK.

Everyone breathed a sigh of relief . . . before fuming at him.

"You jerk!" Max said, catching her breath.

"Not cool," Erica remarked.

"Could have given me a heart attack!" Dustin said.

"No way," Robin chimed in, pretending to clutch her heart. "Get in line, I'm going to the ER first."

The others slowly made their way back to their individual spots in the store, griping about Mike's prank. "Just for that, it's your turn," Lucas said, tossing Mike the flashlight.

Dustin took his hat off to fan himself. "Keep your hands

where we can see them, Mike." Then he added: "I swear, after a night like tonight, I'll have to sleep with the lights on and my teddy bear."

"Big of you to admit you still sleep with a teddy bear, Henderson," Steve said.

Before Dustin could respond to that, Mike clicked the flashlight back on. "A teddy bear, huh? I wouldn't sleep with one if I were you. They're all cute and cuddly one minute, and then before you know it, you hear them . . ."

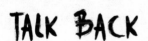

TALK BACK

Shane knew the commercial well. So did his sister, Shawna.

"*Teddy Talkback actually TALKS!*" the announcer would say as the scene showed a teddy bear coming to life in a little girl's bedroom. "*Teddy tells stories, Teddy tells jokes, Teddy talks back . . .*"

"*Good night, Teddy Talkback,*" the little girl would say. "*I love you!*"

"*I love you too*" the teddy bear would reply. Its eyes blinked.

169

Its mouth moved in perfect sync with the words. It looked like it was actually alive! *"Now close your eyes and rest your head. It's time for you to go to bed . . ."*

The commercial ended with the little girl's parents turning out the lights as she cuddled under the covers with her Teddy Talkback. When the bear's heart was pressed, it played a lullaby, which made its chest glow softly like a night-light. The announcer's booming voice would return to let you know which toy stores carried Teddy, and that the pleasure of his cuddly company would cost you *"just 129.99!"* It was the hottest toy at Christmastime three years running. Every kid of a certain age owned one.

Shawna only had hers three months before she died.

She had been sick for a long while before that. The family watched her deteriorate a little more each day, powerless to stop it. And though they had always known the worst was around the corner, nothing could have prepared them to say goodbye. Especially Shane. Normally, two years is quite the age gap for siblings, but Shane and Shawna had always been close. They walked to and from school each day and watched cartoons together for hours instead of doing their homework.

Which meant they knew some TV commercials and jingles the way rocket scientists knew rockets.

Mr. Owl, the Kool-Aid Man, and especially Teddy Talkback were burned into their brains.

Shawna would always light up when that Teddy Talkback ad came on. And Shane, being a good big brother, saw how much joy Teddy brought her and decided to do something about it. He told his parents that Shawna wanted one for Christmas more than anything else, and he even volunteered to kick in his allowance to help them pay for it.

Despite the mounting hospital bills and medication costs, Shane and his parents were able to gift-wrap a Teddy Talkback for Shawna under the tree that holiday.

Her last holiday.

She was happy . . . for a moment, Shane thought, staring at the abandoned Teddy Talkback on the windowsill in Shawna's bedroom. The bear's animatronic eyelids were closed and it sat limply, arms at its sides, head bowed down, like it too was in mourning. "'Teddy tells stories, Teddy tells jokes,'" Shane said, quoting the commercial. "Tell me a joke now, Teddy."

Silence.

"Say something, dammit." Shane pressed Teddy's chest.

No response. Just clicks.

Shane gave Teddy a shake. The motion made the doll's eyelids roll back for a moment before closing again. He turned the bear over and lifted its red and gold vest. There, in the fur, was a little clip to lift its back hatch. Shane opened and saw that the batteries inside had corroded over with hard, white acid. He popped them out into his palm and walked to the kitchen for a replacement.

In the hallway, he could hear the voices of his mom and dad. Judging by their hushed tone, they were having a very serious conversation. Presumably in secret.

About him.

". . . he's in there again," he heard his dad whisper. "In Shawna's room."

". . . he's getting worse," he heard his mom follow up.

"The Murphys said Kevin invited him to go to his pool party next weekend, and Shane said he couldn't go. Made up some lie about us going out of town."

"I'm worried. I don't want to lose another one . . . ," his mom said, choking up.

Shane stopped and waited in the hallway, eavesdropping from the shadows.

"So what, then? A shrink? We can't afford that. We're still paying for—"

"Shane needs help. All he does is sit in her room, like he's waiting for her to come back. He doesn't even watch TV anymore."

"What are we saying here? That our son is having some sort of—"

"Sort of what?" Shane said, popping into the kitchen. His mom and dad froze, abruptly stopping their conversation.

Dad pretended to go back to reading the paper. Mom's eyes went wide at the sight of Teddy. She stood up and put a loving hand on Shane's shoulder. "Honey, what are you doing with Shawna's Teddy?"

"He needs batteries. These are all used up."

Shane saw his mom and dad exchange a knowing glance.

His mom took the old batteries and tossed them in the trash. "We're not going to be doing that, Shane."

"Why?" Shane asked.

His mom fought back tears. "Because . . . *Shawna* . . . is not here anymore. She doesn't need to talk to Teddy."

"But what about me? I want to talk to Teddy."

"You have real friends your age you can talk to. Not some bear. Now give me Teddy and go play next door at the Murphys."

"But, Mom—"

"Listen to your mother, Shane!" Dad said in a booming voice. "Start acting like a normal kid! Go play ball or ride your bike or something. Just do it outside."

With tears forming in the corners of his eyes, Shane threw Teddy across the room and stormed out.

Later that night, in the darkness, a little light began to glow. And the silence of Shane's house was replaced by a distant chime. It rang alone for a spell and then eventually found its melody. It sounded a lot like an old xylophone recording of "Twinkle, Twinkle, Little Star."

It was coming from Shawna's room.

Shane sat up in bed and peeked into the hallway, seeing a light under Shawna's door. He tiptoed toward her room, expecting to burst in on his parents listening to Shawna's Teddy. The very thing they'd guilted him for! He couldn't wait to see the looks on their faces when he caught them red-handed. But mostly, he couldn't wait to see Teddy perform Shawna's favorite lullaby. Even if it meant his heart would break all over again.

Just as he heard the final chimes of the song play, Shane quickly opened the door and was shocked to find the room completely empty. No Mom. No Dad. Only Teddy, propped up on Shawna's bed.

With its eyes open.

The red glow coming from Teddy Talkback's heart-shaped chest-light gave the room an eerie feel. Shadows covered the walls. The floor seemed like an island in an inky void.

175

Shane sat on Shawna's bed, gazing into Teddy Talkback's hazel eyes. After a few moments, it blinked.

"Mom must have replaced the batteries after all," Shane said out loud, talking to himself.

He popped open Teddy's chest, revealing a cassette tape inside. This was how the bear spoke and sang. A cassette of dozens of prerecorded sayings and tunes made it seem like Teddy had an answer for everything, and a song for every occasion.

Shane took out the tape, expecting to see the "Twinkle, Twinkle, Little Star" demo. But to his astonishment, it was an unmarked, homemade tape with the label rubbed off.

"That's weird," Shane said, puzzled. He flipped Teddy over, popped open the battery hatch, and gasped. There were no batteries.

"Shane?" a little voice asked, startling him.

He dropped Teddy, and saw that the power button was switched off. And yet somehow, a voice came out of Teddy's mouth again, saying "Shane?"

It can't be, Shane thought. *I'm dreaming. This isn't real.*

176

Teddy's not talking. Get a grip, Shane.

Shane returned to the door, about to twist the knob, when he heard the little voice again. "Shane?"

He spun around to see Teddy propped back up against the pillows in a seated position. The little bear's eyes and mouth suddenly started moving in perfect sync, asking once more: "Shane?"

Shane felt his knees go weak.

"Listen to me very carefully," Teddy Talkback said. "Don't be frightened."

"What?" Shane asked, unable to believe what was happening. "Can you see me, Teddy?"

"Yes. And I'm not Teddy." The bear stood slowly. It started walking on its own to the edge of the bed. "It's me, Shane . . . it's Shawna."

Shane couldn't help it. He was so overwhelmed, the tears came.

The talking teddy bear climbed off the bed and onto the floor. As it came toward Shane, it reached out its furry paw to comfort him. "Don't worry, I'll never leave you again. Never *ever*."

Over the next few days, Shane was very careful not to be seen going to and from Shawna's room to visit Teddy. He'd pick his moments—usually late at night after his parents had fallen asleep or in that sweet spot after school where he had the entire house to himself for an hour. Much to his surprise, the bear was always awake, waiting for him at the door, ready to be picked up. Ready to talk. Ready to spend time with him.

Just like Shawna.

To Shane's knowledge, Teddy played dead most of the day, to avoid being seen, or worse, caught, by Mom and Dad. The bear had an uncanny ability to turn off and go limp at the slightest hint of noise.

"Where do you go, when you do that? When you turn off?" Shane asked it.

Teddy didn't like questions like these, let alone the bigger, philosophical kind that Shane brought up from time to time instead of letting the bear read him a story or sing him a song. *Is*

your soul trapped in there, Shawna? Or are you communicating with me through the bear . . . from somewhere else? Shane was desperate to understand how any of this was possible.

Teddy would just furrow his furry little brow when these questions came up, giving the impression of having "a serious face."

"I don't have all the answers, Shane," Teddy told him. "Let's just enjoy our time together." Then the cassette tape inside its chest would start playing, slow and garbled at first, eventually warping into a sound closer to the factory recording. In a prerecorded way, Teddy would then mechanically blurt out, "Now, who wants a lullaby?"

Shane would just let the nursery rhyme play, sometimes to remind him of Shawna, sometimes to give Teddy a few melody-tinged moments to cool off. He didn't want to make Teddy angry. Behind that soft, plushy exterior was an intimidating presence. One that liked to be in control.

Questions were out of its control. Questions were bad.

One Tuesday afternoon, during one of these "lullaby breaks," Shane let his mind wander, remembering Shawna's last days in the hospital bed, surrounded by flowers and games and stuffed animals of every size and color. She had a toy store at her fingertips, and yet she never stopped hugging Teddy.

Teddy was special to her. Shane held that thought, reminding himself of it whenever Teddy made things uncomfortable. Which was happening more and more lately.

Just as the final notes of "Oh! Susanna" chimed out of Teddy's chest, Shane suddenly heard a voice behind him. "Shane? What are you doing in here?"

It was Shane's dad. Home three hours early, but smelling like he'd taken a shower in old beer.

"Dad, you're home early," Shane said in a guilty way, tossing Teddy aside. The bear went limp, letting its eyelids roll open.

So it could watch.

"How many times are we gonna do this, son?" Dad asked, slurring his words a bit. "You have got to stop coming in here. It's not healthy."

Dad elbowed past Shane and grabbed Teddy. Shane tried to protest, but it was no use. "Wait, I can explain—"

Shane's dad ignored him, staring into the bear's eyes with a drunken sadness. "Is this what you've been doing after school lately? You've been hiding in here, having tea parties with this?"

"Dad, you have to listen," Shane said, trying to explain. But his dad was already out the door with Teddy in his hand. He was heading toward the kitchen.

Toward the trash can.

"Dad, wait! Please!" Shane begged.

"This bear is history," his dad said, opening the garbage can. "It should have left when she did." He burst into tears. "It should have gone with her. It shouldn't be hanging around here, making us all miserable. Reminding us that it's here in our house and she isn't."

Shane could see his dad's knuckles going white, tightening around Teddy, trying to crush its machine parts out of pure rage. The plastic made a squeaky sound as his fist clenched.

"Dad, wait! Don't! You're killing her! Shawna's in there!" Shane yelled.

Shane's dad stopped squeezing. A sober look crossed his face during a long, pregnant pause. "What did you just say?"

"Shawna's inside Teddy. She speaks through him, she's not

gone. You can't throw her away. You've got to believe me."

Shane spoke to Teddy. "Please, Teddy, you have to show him. You have to talk."

Silence.

His father's rage spiked once more.

"Is that so?" he asked mockingly. He stared into the bear's lifeless eyes. "Talk to me, honey. Sing a song for Daddy."

Teddy just stared back at the man. Limp.

Dad shook the bear. "Say something to me, you stupid little bear, or I swear to God, you're going into the blender!"

Teddy's eyes rolled back, opening and closing with each shake. "Say something!" Dad grumbled, huffing and puffing from the anger. "That's it. No more games. No more toys."

His dad flipped the lid off the blender and started to mash the stuffed bear inside. Shane tried to stop him. He grabbed for his dad's elbows, trying to pull his arms down, but the old man was much too strong for that. He shoved Shane away and plugged the blender cord into the socket.

"Dad, no! You'll kill her!" Shane screamed.

"*I'm* killing her?" his dad asked in disbelief. "Leukemia killed her. YOU are the one doing the killing around here. You're killing your mother and me when you act like a little nutball, you know that? Hasn't this family been through enough?"

Before Shane's dad could hit the Purée button, the front door opened and he stopped immediately. It was his mom, home from work. She dropped her things to the floor, shocked at the sight of Shane crying and her husband with a teddy bear in the blender.

"What the hell is going on here?" she asked.

Shane ran to her, bawling. "Mom, don't let him do it. Don't let him kill *her.*"

Later that night, Shane lay in bed staring at a comic book. Only he wasn't reading it.

He was trying to focus hard enough to eavesdrop on his parents, who were having an intense argument in the kitchen. About what to do with him.

And about what to do with Teddy. And all the rest of Shawna's things.

It seemed his dad wanted to fully clean out her room and get rid of her stuff to give the family "a fresh start." That went way beyond turning her bedroom into a home office, and felt more like him trying to erase her completely from their lives. Thankfully, by the muffled sounds of his mom's crying, she wanted no part of that plan.

Shane heard her lobby for preserving Shawna's room and instead focusing on ways to help them all get some peace.

Especially Shane.

"He needs help," he heard his mom say. "He needs a change. Maybe some time away will do him some good."

Shane didn't like the sound of that. He'd had friends who were sent to live *someplace else* after their parents called it quits, and it never ended happily. He couldn't hear her exact tone over the noise of a passing garbage truck outside, but he did hear something that broke his heart a little: "Granny's."

They wanted to send him away to live with his granny. In Iowa. They were seriously talking about just giving up on him and dumping him across the country to be someone else's problem for a while.

Granny doesn't even like me, Shane thought. *I'm staying right here, and so is Teddy.*

Shane snapped out of it and felt a panic take hold. *Where was Teddy?*

Shane had lost sight of the bear after his mom whisked him away to his bedroom to calm down. He'd never heard the blender start, so he knew Teddy was fine and in one piece—he just wasn't sure where.

Until he heard the door creak open to his left.

Shane glanced over. It was Teddy, pushing inside and taking cover under the bed.

"We need to leave," he heard Teddy say from the shadows underneath him. "They're going to hurt me."

Shane rolled over, hanging upside down to get a look at the little bear hiding under the boxspring. Only its eyes were visible, reflecting the lamplight the way a real animal's eyes would glow at night.

"Where have you been?" Shane asked.

"Your mom had me on the couch for a while," Teddy replied. "I heard everything. They want to send you away. And they want to hurt me."

Shane's heart sank—his choices were becoming grimmer by the second. He knew he needed to make a decision to save them both.

"How do we sneak out?" Shane asked. "And where do we go?"

The little bear crawled forward quietly. "I know a place."

After a short while, when his parents were fast asleep and the entire neighborhood seemed to be at an eerie standstill, Shane snuck out of his house with nothing but his bike at his side and a bookbag on his back. A soft baby-talking voice fed him directions from inside the zipped-up bag. "There's a church by the old Hawkins bridge—take me there. And avoid the main roads. We don't want to be seen."

Shane did as he was told, biking into the darkness.

"I'm scared," Shane admitted.

186

"Would you like me to play you a song?" Teddy asked, slipping into his prerecorded song mode.

"Yes, please. Anything to keep me company."

Just then, "London Bridge" began to play from inside his bookbag. Shane hummed along, taking every back road and shortcut he'd learned from the other boys at school. In his old life. Back when they'd still ask him to come out to play. Shawna's passing had changed all that.

London Bridge is falling down, falling down . . .

Shawna—that was who he was doing this for, risking exile from the family to Iowa.

Falling down . . .

As the spokes turned and the music chimed, Shane realized he no longer heard Teddy Talkback the bear in his ear, he could only hear Shawna singing to him. In a few moments, he'd have his sister back and all this pain and heartache would be over.

London Bridge is falling down, my fair lady . . .

Up ahead, lighting the night like a beacon, was a row of candles burning outside St. Michael's Church. True to what Teddy said, the dusty old house of God was next to another ancient landmark: the old Hawkins bridge.

What Teddy had neglected to mention was that it was also next to a graveyard.

That gave Shane pause as he slowly rode up the path toward the church's front steps.

He set his bike on its side, and when he opened the door, he saw the wide, empty church awaiting them. Vigil candles were lit in each of the windows, giving an ominous fireside tinge to the pews and altars. Shane took a candle, its little light giving him a sense of security in this cold, unknown place.

"Let me out," Teddy said, adding a friendly giggle at the end.

Shane looked around but saw no priests or churchgoers. Besides the eerily lifelike sculptures of Jesus and Mary, the entire place seemed to be theirs, and theirs alone. He unzipped his bookbag and set it down, allowing Teddy to poke his furry head out.

"I've got a surprise for you," Teddy said sweetly.

"Shawna, I want to go home," Shane replied. "I'm scared."

"Don't be scared. How about another little nursery rhyme to help you feel better?"

"Okay."

"First give me your hand," Teddy said in its friendliest,

softest voice. Shane set the candle down on the floor and took Teddy's paw.

Teddy's eyes blinked and moved, slipping into its famous rhyme from the commercial: *"Now close your eyes and rest your head . . ."*

"It's time for you to go to bed," Shane was about to say . . . when something caught his eye at the last second. Something shiny.

Something that glinted in the candlelight like metal.

"It's time for you . . ." Teddy suddenly paused. Then its voice steadily warped and grew deeper. *"To end up DEAD!"*

Slice! Shane winced as Teddy sliced his palm with something very sharp.

"Ow!" Shane yelped, pulling his injured hand back.

Shane now saw the four-cornered object in Teddy's palm. *The blender blade,* he soon realized. *Teddy must have swiped it from the kitchen.*

"You want to see Shawna again, right?" Teddy Talkback asked. "I can grant you that wish."

Shane recoiled, stunned, as Teddy came toward him with the star-shaped blade in its paw. The bear did away with prerecorded messages and baby talk. The robotic blinking was over. Now its eyes remained open with a cold, vacant death-stare.

It began speaking in gibberish. *"NUNC TE FALLAT ET REQUIESCAM . . ."*

Whatever life force was inside Teddy, whatever was speaking *through him* at that moment, it was clear that it wasn't human. This wasn't Shawna's voice trying to communicate from the Great Beyond, this was something else, something darker.

An evil force drawn to loss and sadness—one that fed on souls and stole children.

"Help!" screamed Shane, trying to stop the bleeding from his hand. "Somebody help me!"

"TERMINUS SURSUM MORTUUS . . ."

No one was coming to help. If there were priests who worshipped here, they were elsewhere at this late hour. There were no neighbors to hear Shane's cries. Only the echoes from the abandoned bridge on one side and the dead in the cemetery on the other.

He didn't have a prayer.

Feeling the stinging pain in his palm, Shane squeezed his

hand and backed down an aisle. He looked for anything he could use to defend himself, but there were only old paper hymnals.

With the tall, wooden backs of the pews on either side, Shane was trapped between the wall and Teddy Talkback at the end of the aisle. The bear continued stalking toward him, blade out. Reciting the same, garbled incantation: *"NUNC TE FALLAT ET REQUIESCAM . . ."*

Shane could backpedal no more—if he wanted out, he'd have to go through Teddy.

He charged forward and leapt over Teddy, stumbling a bit when he felt another sharp slice through his jeans. The blender blade caught him on the jump.

Shane cried out again to the holy statues and got no answer. He tried to stand and run but couldn't. He was in too much pain to put weight on his leg. He had no choice but to army-crawl toward the front doors.

Toward the vigil candle he'd left on the floor. Its flame flickered—sparking an idea.

Shane crawled through the pain and released his injured hand in time to grab the candle—just as Teddy leapt onto his back.

"Good night, Shane," Teddy said, raising the blender blade.

"Time for *YOU* to go to bed!" Shane shot back, lifting the candle straight up into Teddy's chest. A quick burst of flame covered the bear, igniting the faux fur in moments. As the fire grew, the bear screamed in agony. Its voice deepened and slowly died, making its shriek sound otherworldly, like the cry of some wounded animal.

Like it could feel the pain of being burned *alive*.

Months passed, making that fateful night in the church feel like a distant nightmare.

The snow came, and the lights went up in downtown Hawkins, marking the beginning of the annual winter holiday festivities. Shane was actually looking forward to Christmas this year, since he'd be spending it at home, with his mom and dad, who were now healing in their own way and trying to act more like a regular family.

Therapy was helping them get there.

As were the game nights spent with neighbors. And the weekend spent decorating the tree. And the Friday nights out for pizza.

On one chilly Friday, Shane and his parents ducked into the warmth of a Pizza Hut for their usual deep-dish escape. While his dad told a few corny jokes and his mom did her best to tease about the presents stashed under the tree, all Shane could do was silently stare out the window.

Past the shoppers and kids hauling sleds.

Across the street . . . to the front window of a toy store, lit up with blinking red and green lights. There, on display for holiday shoppers, was a selection of brand-new Teddy Talkbacks. The boxes were stacked on top of one another in an eye-catching pyramid shape. Next to them—almost standing watch—was an animatronic standee sign of a giant Teddy. Its eyes slowly blinked and its hand waved. A glittery sign overhead read TEDDY SINGS CAROLS, TEDDY TELLS STORIES, TEDDY TALKS MORE . . . THAN EVER BEFORE!

Shane felt the hair on the back of his neck stand up. He mindlessly ran his finger over the scar on his palm. It was a nervous tic he'd recently picked up—not unlike nailbiting. It was all he could do to not freak out as he watched family after family exit the store wearing smiles, all with Teddy Talkbacks tucked under their arms.

The bears were on their way to homes all across town. All across the state. Maybe even the country.

Shane neglected his pizza and tuned the world out, lost in thought. Shawna's Teddy had been destroyed—he was certain of it. He had watched it burn to a smoldering, melting blob. There was no coming back from that level of destruction. Surely the evil inside it had been destroyed too?

"Shane, something wrong?" his mom asked.

"Shane?" his dad added, getting concerned.

Silence.

He wasn't ignoring them. He just couldn't hear them over the nagging feeling inside.

The feeling that it wasn't truly over.

The fear that the evil wasn't really gone.

It was impossible to know if what had happened with Shawna's Teddy would ever happen again. Shane felt the scar, peering into the lifeless black eyes of the Teddy standee across the street. Was it looking back at him? Or was it his imagination?

He shuddered at the thought. Then, like an earworm, his brain began to replay Teddy's eerie rhyme over and over. But the more he recited it, the more he changed the words.

Now close your eyes and rest your head . . .

As long as Teddy's out there . . . evil's not dead.

IN A FLASH

Mike clicked the flashlight off, once again shrouding the store in darkness.

"You know, if tonight was a scary story that we were all somehow in, this is when the freaky reveal would happen," Max said. "Like Nancy would find a killer's hook hanging on the front door, or Steve would announce he was an axe murderer this whole time, or you know, random lights would start flashing—"

Just then, red and blue flashes lit up the street outside, startling the kids—followed by the familiar wail of police sirens. They all rushed to the front windows to see a convoy of Hawkins cop cars speed by, doing at least sixty-five.

"Where do you suppose they're headed?" Mike asked, his hands cupped around his eyes in an attempt to see through the glass he was fogging up.

"Pennhurst," Nancy said. "It's just up the road, remember?"

Mike, Dustin, Lucas, Erica, and Max each looked over at her, mouths open in fright.

Then chaos erupted, with a flash. Then another. And another.

The overhead fluorescent lights were turning back on, blinding the kids with a series of bright lights. They all had to squint while their eyes adjusted. With a static pop, the appliances all came to life, too. The TV monitor flashed the familiar blue screen of Channel 3. The squiggly sounds of VCRs could be heard as the machines resumed rewinding tapes. Clocks flashed 12:00. And the bulb in the popcorn machine hummed on.

As if on cue, the world outside lit up, too—the Palace Arcade sign flickered on over the parking lot.

Nancy changed the channel on the TV, switching over to the news. On-screen, a reporter stood outside Pennhurst Asylum. A yellow line of crime scene tape was being unfurled behind her.

Nancy turned the volume up as everyone in the store crowded around to watch.

"A town in the dark as shocking news comes to light," the reporter said. "Police believe tonight's blackout was no accident, and they're asking for your help to track down a suspicious person believed to have tampered with parts of the power grid in an effort to help a deranged maniac escape custody under cover of night."

The screen cut to a police sketch of a man whose face ominously lacked detail in the drawing, looking less like a person and more like a human being wearing a mask. The reporter continued, "Police are on the lookout for this man, who made a daring escape from Pennhurst Asylum earlier this evening—"

Just then, the TV flipped back to the blue screen, leaving everyone stunned and silently freaking out.

"Hey," Steve said with the remote in his hand. "This is gonna sound kinda funny, but . . . did anyone else feel a little better *before* all the lights came back on?"

A chorus of yesses filled the store. As did the familiar cover of shadows.

"I choose darkness," Robin said.

"Me too," Mike added.

The others agreed: "Same here." "Me too." "Keep 'em off."

They sat back down, each claiming their spots on the floor, already feeling safer. No one was in a rush to get home, or see the sun, or venture out too soon—not while the man on the news was out there. Not while the unknown, on the other side of the glass, was waiting for them.

After all, anything could happen out there. Living in Hawkins was scary enough.

THE END